WAR GAMES

For the children and grandchildren of Charles, William, Jenny, Penny and Jonathan Chadwick, and to Gerda Mayer and Miriam Hodgson with gratitude and love.

WAR GAMES

Jenny Koralek

EGMONT

Acknowledgements

The sources of some of the facts in this story were taken from Miss D Warriner's Report which forms part of the R J Stopford Papers in the Department of Documents at the Imperial War Museum, London, some transcripts from Pathé News, April 1945, *We Came As Children* (ed. Karen Gershon, Gollancz, 1966), *How We Lived Then* by Norman Longmate (Hutchinson, 1971), and *The Poetry Review* [requiem for the twentieth century], Vol. 88, No. 4, Winter 1998/99, p. 25, Gerda Mayer on her flight to England.

First published in Great Britain 2002
by Egmont Books Limited
239 Kensington High Street
London W8 6SA

Text copyright © 2002 Jenny Koralek
Cover design copyright © 2002 Paul Catherall

The moral rights of the author and the cover illustrator have been asserted

ISBN 1 4052 0074 X

10 9 8 7 6 5 4 3 2 1

A CIP catalogue record for this title is available from the British Library

Typeset by Avon DataSet Ltd, Bidford on Avon, Warwickshire B50 4JH
Printed and bound in Great Britain by Cox & Wyman Ltd, Reading, Berkshire

Contents

Part One: Hugo

Part Two: Holly

Part Three: Holly and Hugo

Part One

Hugo

1

Hitler's coming

February 1939 and somewhere in the city of Prague, among its old red roofs and cobbled streets, a boy lay ill.

There was snow on the ground, every bit as deep and crisp and even as it was when good King Wenceslas reigned over the land.

The great castle loomed high on its hill, spiked with icicles.

Slender Christian spires stood out against the deep blue of the sky.

And in the old Jewish ghetto the clock with the Hebrew numbers on it marked the hours backwards, yet could not turn time backwards.

Some children were having a snowball fight in the little park by the wide slow-flowing River Vltava. Others were whizzing on wooden sledges down the slopes below the bell-filled cupolas and the pink and white icing-sugar walls of a convent.

But Hugo Altman lay full of fever in his warm dark room beneath his goosedown quilt, hearing yet not hearing, neither awake nor asleep, yet strangely alert.

His mother was sitting by him. She was always there whenever he woke. Always there to persuade him to take a sip of the honeyed lemon drink she makes fresh for him every day. Always there with gentle words which soothe him as she changes the cold compresses to make his head ache less.

Suddenly through his foggy misery Hugo sensed a new tension in the room. He knew without opening his eyes that his father was there, at the foot of the bed.

'What are you doing at home in the middle of the day?' his mother asked.

'I will tell you. I will tell you.' His father sounded desperately worried. 'But first . . . how is he? Poor child. Please God he turns the corner soon. Did he take any soup today? We must get him better quickly. It is the wrong moment to be ill. I've just heard terrible news.'

'Ssh!' his mother whispered fiercely. 'Do you want to waken the boy? Do you want to frighten him? So! What is this "terrible news"?'

'We're next.'

'Next? What do you mean, we're next?'

'*We* are. This country . . . next to join the Nazi circle . . . I took a good customer into the Hotel Alcron for a drink just now. A group of Germans were moving away from the bar.

They were laughing! Laughing among themselves. So when I was paying for our beers I asked Franz – you know, the barman, Franz – what the joke was. He was so white, so pale and his hands were trembling. "Bohemia's next," he muttered, only just able to look me in the eye. "That's what they were saying . . . Bohemia's next in their Nazi round-up . . ." "When?" I asked him. "March," he said, white as a sheet. "Middle of March at the latest . . ."'

'Oh, my God!' Hugo heard his mother's gasp. 'That's only a few weeks away! Oh, God!'

We're next . . . Bohemia's next in the Nazi round-up . . . March . . . middle of March at the latest . . .

The words began a frenzied dance in Hugo's aching head.

'We've got to get out and fast,' his father was saying. 'And if not us, at least the child . . .'

A silence was in the room, a silence so chill Hugo thought for a moment that his quilt must have fallen off the bed.

But no, the chill was inside his hot, hot body. *Get out . . . at least the child . . .*

'No! No! You cannot part me from him!'

'Oh, my darling! Please God it will not come to that! But we must go to all the consulates in Prague to try for visas – for anywhere! Chile, Australia, England, Venezuela, Canada – it does not matter where. Anywhere as long as we can get out of here before . . . before it is too late!'

'Ssh! Ssh!'

5

Hugo heard his mother choking back a sob. 'Please take this compress . . . take my place . . . I must get out of here for a few minutes . . .'

His father bent over heavily, more clumsily than his mother, placing the fresh cold compress over his head so lovingly, then pulling the feather quilt closer to his chin, tucking it in under his toes as he always did when he came to say goodnight.

'Sleep on,' he whispered. 'Get well. Strong. God alone knows what we have in front of us now.'

He crept away and when he opened the door Hugo could hear his mother crying in the kitchen.

And when the door was closed again, Hugo lay frozen, pressed deep into the mattress, knowing that this was not a bad dream coming from his illness, but a nightmare. Was it possible to have a nightmare when you know you are wide awake?

2
The Englishmen

Hugo did get better.

As soon as he was on his feet again, thin and still weak, he began a daily trudge with his parents from consulate to consulate.

In spite of the cold and the now dirty snow, his mother insisted Hugo and his father wear their best thin black leather shoes, which she made them polish nightly. She herself wore her best felt hat with its jaunty feather and high-heeled shoes and silk stockings, even though they were soon mud-splashed up to the hem of her skirt.

Day after day they sat in grand, high-ceilinged rooms and waited, filled in forms, answered questions, and waited, only to be turned away again and again without the papers needed to take them to safety.

Safety. Safety from what? Hugo never dared to ask his parents outright. He guessed it was something too terrible to ask about. He felt more and more left out as his parents increasingly broke off their low-voiced conversations, or hurriedly put the phone down whenever he entered a room.

The day came when there were no more consulates to go to and his father, a jeweller and watchmaker, returned to his shop in the smartest street in the city.

His mother started leaving him with their maid, while she went out for long hours, returning exhausted, tense and irritable. Hugo would hear her in the kitchen, banging saucepans and muttering: 'Unbelievable! Incredible! All quotas filled!' But when he asked her what she meant and what was happening, she only stroked his hair and made soothing sounds: '*Na*! *Na*! It is nothing. Don't worry. Go down to the courtyard, my darling, and play . . .'

Then one afternoon she came running into his room wearing her best hat.

'A miracle! A miracle!' she cried. 'Come, Hugo! Come! Quickly! Get your coat on! I have told your father already – there is an Englishman! Oh, Hugo, he is going to help us!' And burst into tears.

Hugging him, she wiped her eyes, and helped him into his coat. Then they fetched his father from the shop and hurried, all three, to a grand hotel to meet the Englishman.

In fact two Englishmen were watching out for them near the revolving door and quickly came towards them as they entered.

The taller one took command at once.

His hair was a flame of red-gold, his eyes deep blue. He looked as if he laughed and smiled often. *He* wasn't wearing a smart suit and shiny shoes, Hugo noticed at once. *He* was wearing a shabby dark blue jersey and old baggy trousers. Hugo thought he looked like a god in disguise.

'Hello,' he said, coming forward briskly. 'I'm Miles Nash and this is my brother, Guy.'

They all shook hands, but even as they did so Miles Nash was leading them to a quiet corner and urging them to sit down.

The soft leather armchairs were the kind to sink back into, but the Altmans sat nervously on the edge, their backs stiff, straining anxiously in the effort to understand the Englishman's poor German.

'We don't have much time, I'm afraid,' he said slowly, searching for each word. 'But what is important is that we have the "guarantors" . . . "sponsors" – our parents, you understand? Our father and mother. They have signed the necessary documents. So it is certain there are no problems. You have the photos, the birth certificate?'

Hugo's parents nodded eagerly. His mother handed over passport photos and papers.

The grown-ups talked for a while, struggling in the English and German they had learnt at school long ago.

'Soon,' Hugo heard Miles say. 'Maybe tomorrow even. Go home. Get everything ready. Wait by the phone.'

9

Then he turned to Hugo and smiled at him. His smile was kind, but his eyes were sad.

'*Auf Wiedersehen, Hugo,*' he said in his strange accent. '*Auf Wiedersehen*, until we meet again.'

'*Auf Wiedersehen*,' said Hugo politely.

'Thank you, thank you!' his mother gushed, clasping the Englishmen in turn by the hand.

'Yes,' said his father more quietly, a tremble in his voice. 'Thank you and . . . *Wiedersehen*.'

And as Hugo followed his parents through the hotel doors he suddenly understood.

'It's me,' he said, tugging at his father's coat sleeve. 'It's me, isn't it, who's going to go somewhere with these men? Tell me! Tell me, what's going to happen to me . . . to us?'

Looking up into their faces he was frightened by the tears in their eyes as they exchanged anxious glances.

'Yes, Hugo my darling! We *will* tell you,' said his mother. 'We'll go now to *The Golden Crown* and have a really good talk.'

They found a quiet table in a corner of their favourite café. His parents ordered coffee for themselves and chose for Hugo the pastry they knew he loved best. And then, they both tried to explain.

'There is this terrible man, Hitler . . .'

'Germany's leader . . . and he's coming here soon, very soon . . .'

'He's coming with his army, unwanted, into our country . . .'

'And . . . he hates Jews. He has already shut down their shops in Germany . . .'

'And does not allow them to buy decent food . . .'

'Or sit in the park . . .'

'Or ride their bicycles . . .'

'He has burned down synagogues . . .'

'Thrown them out of schools and stopped them from having jobs, so they can't earn any money . . .'

'Even . . .' his mother put in hesitantly, 'even made them get down on their hands and knees and scrub the pavements . . .'

'Yes,' said his father, 'he is making life impossible for them in every kind of way . . .'

'And now he will come and do the same in Czechoslovakia. He will put Jews in prison . . . in special camps even. Make them do all kinds of hard and dirty work . . .'

'That is why we have been trying to get the necessary papers for us to leave before he comes. But, as you know, we have not succeeded . . .'

'And now this miracle has happened! Kind people from other countries are trying to help children have a chance to escape . . .'

'And these brothers Nash have come all the way from England to take children there to stay with other good

11

people – like a holiday – until their own mothers and fathers can come and fetch them again . . .'

'A plane will be coming to take you to England with about twenty other children either tomorrow or the next day . . .'

'It will be exciting!' said his mother.

'An adventure!' said his father.

'Truly, like a holiday!'

'And you are specially lucky, Hugo, as you will be going to Mr Nash's own mother and father! He promised us that. And there will be other children to play with . . .'

'And we will be coming as soon as we can . . .'

Hugo listened and was afraid, but one look at the fresh tears in his parents' eyes, one glimpse of the determined smiles on their faces, told him that he must not let them know.

'Yes,' he said as brightly as he could. 'Yes, it does sound like an adventure, really . . . I'm beginning to feel quite excited!'

'Good boy,' said his father.

'And now eat up!' said his mother, pulling on her gloves, hunting for her purse. 'We should be getting home.'

Hugo obeyed. But how could something usually so sweet, so creamy, so utterly delicious have suddenly turned so sour, so tasteless and so gritty in his dry mouth?

3
Night flight

That night, long after he had gone to bed, the sound of the phone woke Hugo.

He crept out of bed and saw his mother and father embracing in the hall. Quickly he got back into bed and buried his head, shivering, under the goosefeather quilt.

The next thing he knew it was early morning and his mother was opening his bedroom door.

Then his father was sitting down heavily on the bed, patting his head.

'Come, touslehead,' he said softly. 'It is time.'

Hugo opened his eyes and saw that both his parents were already dressed in their outdoor clothes.

They had brought him hot chocolate and a soft white roll, but he could only manage a few sips, a few mouthfuls.

They made him put on the trousers he usually wore in the mountains for winter sports; his thickest shirt, his warmest jersey; his winter coat and his hat with the earflaps. He was stifled.

Suddenly his father hugged him tight.

'Hugo,' he said, 'you know that we must send you away. Now. Today. Mr Nash and his brother are good men. They will take you far away, to England, where it is safe and where you need not be ashamed or afraid any more of being a Jew. We cannot come with you now. We cannot. But we *will* come. We *will* . . .'

He could not go on. He had to turn away.

'Oh yes!' his mother said fiercely, as she stroked Hugo's hair, buttoning a button. 'And *soon*.'

But she, too, turned away and went to the window, lifting the long, fine lace curtains a little.

'The car is here,' she said softly.

'We must go then,' said his father.

He put an envelope into Hugo's pocket.

'I want you to give this to Mr Nash or to his father or mother. Ask them to keep it safe until . . . until . . .'

'Until things are better again,' his mother said firmly.

His father picked up the little suitcase.

His mother smiled at Hugo.

'Don't worry, my darling,' she said. 'It is not just socks and shirts. Your *Putzi-Leute* are all there in their box. They will not break. I have wrapped each one in cotton wool.' Hugo's 'little people' were his glass and china dogs, ducks, monkeys, swans, piglets, trolls and pixies. They were the

14

souvenirs from holidays, the gifts for no special reason, which he played with nearly every day. 'Those you can play with wherever you are.'

The Altmans were driven beyond the tramlines and the city lights to the airport by a silent man – neither friendly nor unfriendly – concentrating grimly on the icy road. Once they skidded slightly. Hugo was not even scared. He felt as if he were in a dream, not able to make anything happen or stop anything from happening.

He wanted to speak, to ask his parents a thousand questions, but now he could not say a word. He knew, too, that if he did he would cry and so would they.

At last the car stopped outside the entrance to the small airport. It was very quiet and very cold. The Altmans hurried into the departure hall and joined the group of anxious-looking families. Hugo stared at the other children. Some seemed quite excited, but others were whimpering or silent. He edged closer to his father and mother. He gazed back at the entrance, out into the cold, grey, early-morning light. The car wasn't there any more.

Miles Nash stood among the families with his brother, checking names off a list, lining the children up near some glass doors through which Hugo could see a few planes. Mr Nash looked up from his papers and said gently, 'Time to go!' He explained in his bad German that the parents must say goodbye now, that they could not come with the children any further.

Hugo turned to his father and buried himself in his thick coat. His father ran his fingers through Hugo's soft black curls and kissed him. 'Goodbye, Hugo,' he whispered. 'Always do the right thing. For our sakes. For the sake of all Jews. *Wiedersehen*, Hugo. *Wiedersehen* . . .'

Hugo tore his eyes away from his father's sad face and flung himself at his mother. She held him close. How warm she was, how soft her coat was. How soft her cheeks. How lovely her scent, how tender her hands and her last kiss. 'Mr Nash and his brother will take care of you and take you to their parents. *Sei brav, sei gut, mein* Hugo . . . be brave . . . be good . . . And don't forget to brush your teeth, and however strange the food may seem eat it and be thankful. Soon, soon we will all be together again. We want you to be safe.' On that last word she shook him gently to make him let go. But her hands went out to him again, then fell helplessly to her sides. His father laid an arm across his shoulder briefly. Then they stood back and signalled to him: he must go now.

The only adults allowed through the glass doors were a young couple with a baby. The father carried it while the mother held on to its little fat fingers. She was crying silently, but the baby was laughing, even when they handed it to Miles and left.

The children were hurried up the steps and on to the plane. Miles and his brother settled them quickly into their seats and handed out sweets and chocolate.

Some of the children were crying. An older girl said, 'Try

not to cry. This is a great adventure! And we'll be safe in England! England is far away from camps and people hating us. Hitler will never get there. England is an island. You all know what an island is! Surrounded by water. Safe . . .' Her voice wobbled. 'Let's try and get some sleep, or look out of the window . . . see? We're coming out of the clouds now! And there's the sun! Don't eat too much chocolate or you'll be sick! Don't cry! Come on! It'll all be all right. You'll see. You'll see . . . and look! The baby's fast asleep!'

The baby stayed asleep in Miles's lap all through the long journey, even when the plane landed briefly in Holland to refuel.

Hugo was very warm in all his clothes, but his heart was icicle cold.

He had never felt alone till now.

He shut his eyes, and dozed and was sick into a little paper bag, and dozed again.

4
No going back

By the time the plane landed in England, Hugo was exhausted. Miles Nash tucked him up in a rug on the back seat of his car.

'Sleep,' he said. 'It is a long drive to Swanstown . . .'

But Hugo could not sleep.

In the fug of the car – the Nash brothers had both lit up cigarettes – silently Hugo wept.

He wanted to go home. Now. To be there at once.

But it was too late.

England is an island.

How many times his father had told him that, and then that big girl on the plane. He, in the air, had crossed water. There was no way to go back.

In a blur, through the steamy windows he saw houses and streets which could not have looked more different from Prague.

It began to grow dark quickly. He had no idea what time it was, and his head ached.

As they drove on and on, Hugo became aware that they were in the country now. They passed fields where he could make out the shapes of cows and horses. The roads grew narrow and were now lined with ghostly leafless trees.

At some point Guy Nash turned round. He must have seen Hugo's tears for he said something which sounded kind: *Cheerupboy. Soonbetherenow. Hungry? Thirsty?*

These last two words Hugo sort of understood as they sounded close to the German, *hungrig, durstig*.

He nodded – more to be friendly than anything else. He really did not know if he wanted to eat or drink. However, when they stopped at a roadside café he was glad to drink something hot called Ovaltine and nibble at some sweet thing called biscuit.

Soon after that they entered a dark forest. He felt a little better and peering through the window saw ponies beneath the trees.

'New Forest!' Guy informed him. '*Neue Wald*!' he repeated in German. '*Neue Wald, Alte Wald*!' he joked. 'New Forest, Old Forest, New Forest, like your synagogue in Prague . . .'

Hugo smiled at Guy. So he knew about the Old New Synagogue built hundreds of years ago, and was trying to explain to him that this 'new' forest too was old! For a brief moment Hugo felt warm and human again. But it did not last. A chill fell on him and the dark forest suddenly seemed sinister and endless.

'Swanstown!' Miles suddenly said over his shoulder.

19

'Home at last! Too dark now but in the morning you will see the sea: *Im Morgen wirst Du das Meer sehen*!'

He pulled up outside a small house with lights blazing from all its windows and helped Hugo, stiff with tiredness and shyness, out of the car just as the front door opened and a pretty young woman came out.

Guy Nash leapt out of the car and kissed and hugged her. '*Thereyou areatlast poorkid must be exhausted*,' said the pretty young woman, and she gave Hugo a sort of dry peck of a kiss. Then she took him awkwardly by the arm and hand and drew him into the house into a room with an open fireplace where a small fire burned – the first he had ever seen. In Prague there were fat radiators or huge beautiful tiled stoves . . .

'Bed!' said Miles. 'Bed for this boy.'

Pointing to Guy Nash and then back to herself, the woman said to Hugo, 'I am Mrs Nash.'

Then she led him to a table and pointed to a glass of milk and some bread and butter slices.

'Eat?' she half asked, half ordered. 'Drink?'

Shyly Hugo sat down on the edge of a chair and sipped and nibbled.

The grown-ups turned away and stood round the fire as if not wanting to embarrass him with stares. Guy Nash poured drinks for them in little glasses and they all took cigarettes from a silver box and started smoking and talking all at the same time.

'Bed!' said Miles to Hugo again. Mrs Nash led him up the stairs and into a narrow, cold room, opened up his little suitcase, fished out his pyjamas and toothbrush, and showed him a cold lavatory down a cold passage, and a washbasin in a cold bathroom nearby, all the time smiling, smiling in an unsmiling way.

She came into the room again when he was in bed beneath the icy sheets and thin blankets, tucked him in and picked up the slippery eiderdown which had fallen to the floor.

'*Lightsout,*' she said. '*Nightnight,*' she said. '*Sleeptight,*' she said.

He must have fallen asleep at once and deeply. When he woke up it was morning. For a second he thought he was at home in his own bed. Why was the room so cold? And where was his goosedown quilt? Then he remembered where he was. The eiderdown had slipped to the floor again, and a dull light was coming through the short flimsy curtains. He felt like crying and burying his head under the bedclothes, but somehow he knew he did not want the pretty lady to see him like that.

He quickly jumped out of bed, crept to the lavatory and the washbasin, and when he was dressed and his hair brushed, sat on the end of the bed. He had no idea what time it was. He felt very hungry and thirsty, but did not dare go downstairs. He sat there for quite a while, his legs dangling, but too frozen in cold misery to get up and draw back the curtains and take a look outside.

Then there was a soft knock at the door.

Hugo jumped. *How to say; Come in?*

After a while the door opened anyway. In came a small, skinny girl with thin blonde plaits. She stood there silently, staring at Hugo with her big grey-blue eyes.

Hugo stared silently back.

And then, at last, the girl pointed to herself and said, '*Guten Tag*, Hugo. I am Holly . . .'

Part two
Holly

5

Leaving Africa

Holly was Guy and Kitty Nash's daughter and she had been sent upstairs to fetch Hugo down to breakfast. She was almost as much a stranger as Hugo to Swanstown and the little cold house.

Only a few weeks ago she had been in Africa on her father's farm, sitting on the verandah beneath the strong blue sky, scuffing the hot red earth between her bare toes. She should have been watering the hollyhocks before the sun got too high, but instead she was eavesdropping.

Eavesdropping on her parents' angrily raised voices floating out to her through the open doors and windows. They had been listening to their wireless set and shooed Holly out when the news came on. Not that she had wanted to listen, as her parents did daily, to crackly voices from far, far away.

'That settles it,' she now heard her father say. 'It's only a matter of time before war breaks out. We're selling up and going home!'

Going home? Holly shivered. *War?* She felt cold all over as if a huge cloud had suddenly covered the African sun.

Going home? But home was here. Home was the farm on the edge of a desert where thorn trees grew and vultures sometimes circled overhead; the bungalow built by her father, surrounded by trees planted by her father, the windmills to pump up the scanty water supply; the shallow reservoir like a huge saucer waiting to receive every precious drop of rain; the garden where her father had once killed a puff-adder uncoiling from the leafy cool of the tomato plants; her father's gentle black and white cows who chomped on mealies and let down warm milk and won him prizes at the local shows.

And surely her mother wouldn't want to leave little brother's grave under the gum trees? Hardly a day went by without the two of them going there with a few fresh flowers . . .

'Sell the farm?' she heard her mother say angrily. 'After all you've put into it? Going home? I thought our home was here!'

Holly could have kissed her mother, but her father took no notice.

'This so-called agreement for peace,' he was saying, 'it won't last. Hitler's not to be trusted, we've had enough proof of that already! There will be a war, no doubt of it. I'm sorry, Kitty, my mind's made up – we're going home.'

'I thought this was our home,' her mother said again, but this time sadly.

Her father blustered on.

'No problem selling it to old Pentz . . . he's been longing to get his hands on my acres and my cows! No, Kitty, I was too young to fight in the last war and I'm damned if I'm going to miss the next one. Besides, this Hitler fellow has got to be stopped . . . He's got a huge army already and a thoroughly modern air force . . . He's only biding his time before he walks all over Europe and the whole world itself. We can't let that happen!'

'And what will you do for a living until this famous war is declared?' said her mother sharply.

'Oh, I'm sure Father will find me some teaching in the old school,' said her father confidently. 'Give me some boys to coach. Have to brush up my Latin and Greek though! If we get on with it we could even be home in Swanstown for Christmas!'

Home in Swanstown, thought Holly indignantly. I don't want to be anywhere but here in our home for Christmas.

All the same, she could not help daydreaming about Christmas in England, which she knew was a cold country where it snowed. And Swanstown was by the sea and she'd never seen the sea. And her grandparents lived there . . . the grandparents she had never met, but who looked very kind and smiling in their photos and who sent her wonderful presents twice a year – Babar books, dolls' clothes, coral beads and the prettiest party dresses.

Suddenly she heard her father coming out on to the

verandah and leapt quickly and guiltily to her feet. She hadn't even filled the watering can.

'Holly!' he said reproachfully. 'What are you doing? Little Miss Big Ears, I suppose!'

But he could never be cross with her for very long.

'Get along now, and water those flowers for your mother!'

Holly knew better than to ask him then and there why he wanted to fight in a war.

But she did not like the picture of this Hitler person 'walking all over the world' as if it belonged just to him. Surely her father was right: he would have to be stopped – and she felt proud that he wanted to help. But it would be dangerous, wouldn't it? Because soldiers get killed, don't they?

6
The ship

They had come out of Africa on a great ship.

In Cape Town, in a cold wind, her mother had pointed out a huge mountain with a flat top.

'It looks like a table,' said Holly. 'And those clouds are like a tablecloth just floating down to settle on it . . .'

'Clever girl!' said her father proudly. 'It is called the Table Mountain!'

On board ship Holly and her mother shared a cabin with a jolly, friendly woman who always wore trousers – 'slacks' she called them – and a lot of make-up.

Her name was Dodo.

'Dodo Church,' she said, 'though anything less like a church than me would be hard to find! Why, before long I hope to become a gay divorcee . . .'

And she laughed loudly.

But Holly didn't think she sounded happy.

'What's a divorcee?' she asked her mother.

'Never you mind,' said Kitty.

But Holly was really only interested in the ship itself: the stuffy, dark cabin, everything bolted to the floor; the neat, narrow bunk beds. You had to climb up a ladder if you wanted to sleep on the top one, which she longed to do, but Kitty wouldn't let her. 'You'll only fall out,' she said briskly.

Holly loved peering out of the round windows, thickly rimmed with brass fittings. She could still see that table-shaped mountain and its tablecloth of clouds. She was puzzled when a steward came in just before they set sail and screwed the portholes tightly shut.

'Why?' she asked.

'You'll find out when we reach the Bay of Biscay, darling!' laughed Dodo.

Holly enjoyed toiling up and down the steep, steep stairs between the decks, and eating huge meals in the grand dining-room lit by glittering crystal lights her mother told her were called chandeliers. She admired the ballroom with its heavy red curtains and a great shiny piano which stood on a platform all to itself.

But best of all Holly liked being up on deck, smooth and wide with acres of space for running, or hiding between the giant lifeboats. Here the air was sharp and new and there were deckchairs where she could stretch out right to the tips of her toes, while her father read to her.

A steward brought them hot drinks served in thick white cups with saucers.

'Don't burn your tongue, darling,' her mother would say, and Auntie Dodo would lean over and blow on the steam in the cup.

The days were long and slow and still warm. It was as if they were all on holiday. Her father joined in the sports on deck and Holly had never seen her mother as full of fun as she became in Dodo's company.

There was even a fancy dress ball. Kitty let Holly help her delve into her cabin trunk from which they fished out two Japanese silk kimonos and two Spanish fans.

Kitty and Dodo did each other's hair up magnificently with tortoiseshell combs.

Holly was allowed to stay up and watch the ball begin. How handsome her father looked with her mother and Auntie Dodo fluttering like beautiful butterflies, one on each side of him, flying off to other dancing partners, but always, one or the other, coming back to him.

But after the ball the weather changed. The sky went grey, the air chilled, the steely waves began to heave themselves into mountains. They had reached the Bay of Biscay.

Holly, Kitty and Dodo were seasick and stayed below for days, nursed in a rough sort of way by a battle-axe of a stewardess. Holly was the first to recover and leave the cabin sickroom.

'Go and find your father,' Kitty said weakly. 'He'll just have to look after you till I'm on my feet again.'

When Holly felt strong enough her father tucked her small hand into his large warm one, and as they walked together round the deck he tried to tell her something about the Nash family. Holly could only catch snatches of what he said, towering above her in the gusts of wind. Something about his brother – 'Terrific chap your Uncle Miles . . . Then there's my sister Constance . . . your Aunt Connie . . . has a daughter . . . surely your mother has told you about your cousin, Imogen?'

Holly tried to tell her father that she hadn't, but the wind blew away her words. Didn't he know her mother did not talk to her much about anything, and certainly not about his family?

'Imogen,' her father rambled on just above her head. 'Must be about your age . . . no, maybe a little older. She'll be someone for you to play with in the holidays . . . she often comes down to Swanstown . . . bit of a tomboy, I gather . . . not surprising I suppose as she goes to some co-ed boarding school. Her father and mother like gadding about . . . have a lot of odd friends who, like them, I regret to say, are pacifists, people who don't believe in fighting wars . . .'

Holly's heart warmed to this unknown aunt and uncle, but she trembled at the thought of having to play with a tomboy cousin.

Altogether she preferred it when her father tucked

her up in a thick rug and read to her from *The House At Pooh Corner*.

The night the ship steamed slowly up the Solent towards Southampton, the foghorns frightened Holly out of her sleep.

'I don't like that noise,' she wept. 'It's so sad it makes me sad . . .'

Kitty stumbled out of bed and hushed her.

'Ssh, ssh! You'll wake Auntie Dodo!' she said. 'Don't be a silly girl. It's a good noise. It's telling the other ships where we are, so we don't collide with them in the fog.'

'I don't want Daddy to be in a war,' Holly sobbed. 'I wish he didn't believe in wars like . . . like . . . Aunt . . . Aunt Connie . . .'

'Oh!' said Kitty irritably. 'What's he been telling you? We think Aunt Connie is silly . . . wrong. Daddy is right to want to fight . . . don't worry, darling. He will be a very brave soldier and anyway I'll be there to take care of you . . .'

But Holly only cried more until Kitty lost patience and tucked her up so tightly in the crisp white sheets and the thin blankets she could hardly move.

'Soon the tugs and the pilot will be out to bring us safely into harbour,' she said briskly, picking up Holly's doll, Mary, and plonking her on to the pillow. 'You'll like the tugs – they're small and cheeky – like toy boats. You'll see them in the morning. Now, go to sleep!'

Holly pressed her hot, damp face against her doll's cold cheek.

'You don't like wars, do you, Mary?' she whispered. 'You don't like that noise either, do you, Mary? It makes you sad, too, doesn't it, Mary?'

7

'Jam in the sandwich'

Guy Nash was the first to spot his parents, Phoebe and Hereward, standing on the dock at Southampton, their solid bodies parting the mists like a pair of sturdy oak trees.

'Wave, Holly, wave!' cried Guy.

He held Holly up to the rail.

'There they are! Your grandparents! Wave! They've seen us now!'

Holly waved at the grandmamma blowing kisses and the grandfather waving his pipe.

They seemed to be wearing a lot of clothes, all green and brown and thick.

Holly fell in love with her grandmamma on sight.

She drank in Phoebe's great smile which made her cheeks ride up and the kind eyes which twinkled with promises of secrets and fun, and flew straight into the outstretched arms. She pressed herself willingly against her and returned the kisses and the incoherent murmurs of welcome with happy little grunts of her own.

Before she knew where she was she was being bundled into the back of her grandfather's car, squashed tightly between Phoebe and Kitty, a rug shared across their knees. Holly leaned happily into her grandmother's soft, full body.

'Jam in the sandwich,' said Phoebe. 'That's what you are, darling, like your Aunt Connie was between your daddy and your Uncle Miles – the jam in the sandwich, that's what I used to say!'

She dived into her large handbag, found barley sugars and offered one to Holly, who lay back sucking happily. She sank so low in her seat that she saw nothing of the road, but dozed, letting her family's words buzz and bumble over her head.

'Old job's waiting for you, Guy!'

'Well, if I can be useful, Dad . . . till war breaks out,' her father replied.

'You can start at once, if you wish,' said her grandfather. 'Robert Pendleton says he'll be only too happy to share the timetable with you . . .'

'Robert Pendleton!' exclaimed Guy. 'Is he still with you?'

'Dear Robert!' said Grandmamma. 'We don't know what we'd do without him!'

She turned to Kitty.

'And you'll be snug at the bottom of the hill in The School Lodge – only a stone's throw away!'

'Thank you, Mamma,' said Kitty. 'Oh! It will be wonderful to have water coming out of taps again!'

'Yes, dear, I expect it will,' said Phoebe. 'I don't know how you managed all those years with . . . er . . . buckets and things . . . such primitive conditions. You wonderful girl!'

'And brother Miles?' Guy interrupted. 'Where is he these days?'

'We-ell,' said Phoebe nervously. 'We don't really *know*, do we, Hereward?'

'He's abroad somewhere,' said Hereward. 'On some fact-finding tour . . . for his newspaper . . .'

'Something to do with refugees,' said Phoebe.

'Refugees?' yawned Kitty. 'What refugees?'

'Jews, I think,' said Phoebe.

Holly wondered sleepily why Grandmamma had lowered her voice suddenly. 'Jews or Socialists, I can't remember which, but *pas devant les enfants*,' she whispered over Holly's head.

Kitty nodded.

Holly turned to Phoebe and asked, 'What's *pas devant*?'

'It's French for not in front of the children,' said Kitty triumphantly. 'You don't need to know about all these things and I don't want to either!'

'France is just over there,' put in Guy, trying to be helpful. 'Over the sea . . .'

He pointed out into the gathering darkness.

'Not so many miles away,' added Hereward, slowing

his car as they drove into the beginnings of a town.

'Only twenty-one miles, in fact, between Dover and Calais,' said Guy.

Holly suddenly felt very tired and rather sick from the smell of her grandfather's pipe.

Phoebe came to the rescue. She leaned forward and tapped the men on the shoulder.

'Listen to you two! A proper pair of schoolmasters burdening this weary child with facts and figures! Really, Guy! Nobody would ever believe you'd been out of the classroom for more than a day!'

'Sorry, Mother,' said Guy. 'Sorry, Holly darling. Poor little mite! You must be ready for bed all right!'

'This is a homecoming!' Phoebe cried out. 'A day for rejoicing!'

She turned to Holly and smoothed her hair and kissed the top of her head. Her diamond and emerald rings glittered on her fine old hands.

'Homey jog,' she crooned. 'Homey jog! Nearly there. These are the lights of Swanstown. What we all need is a nice hot cup of tea . . . and cocoa for you, pet?'

Behind the grown-ups' talk Holly had heard hints of dark things, but she was too tired, just too tired.

Her head fell on to Phoebe's arm against the soft tweed of her sleeve.

Whatever was happening in the world she knew already that Phoebe would never let her come to harm.

8

Imogen

Swanstown-by-the-Sea lay in a crescent of fine sands, edged at both ends by green-haired, whiter-than-white chalk cliffs.

The Nashes' school, The Priory, sat on a hill in the middle of the town. All its many windows faced the bay – windows always open, moist air and salty breezes tugging at the thin curtains and dampening the boys' skimpy bedding, yet somehow never ridding the passages of boot polish and cabbage smell. A great wide white balcony ran the breadth of the first floor where Holly's grandparents had their private rooms surrounded by dormitories and classrooms.

At the bottom of the hill lay Holly's new home, The School Lodge. It was a poky little house. The rooms were small and gloomy, the furniture dark and uncomfortable: nothing but heavy chests and wooden settles, and high-backed chairs with hard seats. Everything seemed to be painted brown. The flowery patterns on the sofas and armchairs were faded and dull; the few pictures were of shaggy cattle with long horns.

Holly's room, the nursery on the top floor, was the only bright room in the house. Its wooden panelling reminded her of the deck on the ship. From the large window she could watch the gulls with their v-shaped wings flapping away in the grey sky. She could see the daily steamer from the big town across the bay sailing slowly into Swanstown's harbour, looking like a toy boat floating on a half moon of water.

There was a fireplace in the nursery with a high fender, a rocking chair, a rocking horse and Babar books.

'I had such fun doing this room up,' her grandmother had said on that first chill night.

She had lit the fire herself, kneeling there a long time, her large bottom in the air, puffing away till she had succeeded in coaxing pale flames out of the damp coal. Then she had undressed Holly beside it, drawn her on to her lap and cradled her, rocked her and lulled her, before tucking her up and staying with her until she fell asleep.

'First night in a strange room,' she had said, beaming her great smile.

The room had been alive with the flicker of flames, the curtains drawn against the dark outside.

There had been a fire downstairs to welcome them too.

Her father had stood in front of it, rocking slightly on his heels, happy to be at home at last, till Kitty asked him to sit down as she couldn't feel any warmth at all.

'I had quite forgotten how cold it is in this country,' she said.

In the morning, when Holly woke up, her grandmother had gone and the fire was out.

The room was bitterly cold.

Holly shivered.

She looked at the other bed. Imogen was coming to stay at Christmas. Grandmamma had told her last night. She would sleep in that bed.

Imogen! The thought of her tomboy cousin filled her with dread.

Christmas was not far off, but she would not think about Imogen until she was standing in front of her.

Meanwhile she made the most of her father's company after lunch when, sticking to African habits, her mother always sent her up to the nursery to rest. A little later Guy would sneak up and lie on Imogen's bed, whispering nonsense rhymes, making animal noises, pretending to snore, laughing softly at her giggling happiness, enjoying their secret.

Then he would creep away, a finger to his lips.

'Ssh! Holly, poppet! Not a word to your mother, eh?'

On Christmas Eve Imogen arrived with her mother, Connie, and her quiet, shy father, Jocelyn.

Holly and Imogen hated each other on sight.

Imogen looked down at Holly with scorn and Holly was

41

terrified of this cousin with the flashing brown eyes, the dark hair cut short like a boy's.

It was a struggle for her to stand up to the gale of Imogen's energy and endless questions.

'When's your birthday?' she demanded, hands on hips.

'N-november,' faltered Holly. 'November the fifth . . .'

'Guy Fawkes!' Imogen jeered. "S'pose you think the fireworks are all for you! Better watch out they don't put you on the bonfire one day! And anyway, I'm six months older than *you*! Can you play French cricket? Can you swim? Can you climb trees? Ropes? Do you know where babies come from? I'll show you in the bath. What's your worst swear word? Mine's . . .'

'Imogen!' warned Connie, with a glance at Kitty's frozen face.

'Do you know French? I know French and German. I can say hello in five languages . . . I'll teach you. Get some paper and a pencil and we'll play schools . . .'

'My writing's not very good yet,' Holly trembled.

'Oh, you're such a boring little girl. I wish Miles would hurry up and come down. He always knows how to make things fun . . .'

But Miles Nash did not come down. That he was still abroad somewhere, was all his parents knew.

On Christmas Day the family went to church and sang *'Peace on Earth, goodwill to men.'*

And afterwards, they all sat under the lighted

Christmas tree smiling on the two children opening their presents.

'Say thank you to Aunt Constance for the lovely Russian dolls!' said Kitty.

'They're not Russian,' said Imogen bossily, 'they're Polish actually . . .'

'And do let her call me Connie,' urged her mother. 'Imogen does . . .'

'Yes,' said Kitty primly. 'So I've noticed. Really, Connie, you're so . . . so . . . modern!'

Holly did not know what modern was, but she liked her aunt – her calm grey eyes, her quiet voice. She wished she had hair like Connie's – red-gold shining hair all piled up. She had seen how long it was when Connie had unpinned it and washed it under the taps when she and Imogen were having a bath.

At lunch Hereward said a short grace before carving the turkey. As he picked up the knife he could not help adding, 'We should thank our Prime Minister for this peaceful Christmas. If ever there was a day in the year when "peace in our time" means something, it is surely today.'

'It's "peace *for* our time",' said Phoebe rather impatiently. 'Not "peace *in* our time" – you're muddling it up with the prayer book. Don't let the meat get cold, dear,' she added.

'Huh!' growled Guy. 'If you want my opinion, if the old

man had been honest, he'd have said peace for *a* time . . . and a short time at that.'

Holly had pricked up her ears anxiously at her father's words.

'Ssh, Guy!' Phoebe now said. 'Don't let's spoil this happy day!'

Miles had sent Holly a notebook. It was covered in green leather with marbled endpapers and a green silk ribbon to mark the page and its own small pencil tucked into its spine. The pages were unlined.

He had given Imogen a sailing ship in a bottle.

Kitty sent the children into another room to play.

As soon as they were alone Imogen started bossing Holly about.

'Now you've got a notebook we can do vocab . . . go on! Write down *bonjour*! That's French for hello . . .'

'What's *pas devant*?' Holly asked.

She got no further.

'*Pas devant les enfants*,' said Imogen, mimicking their grandmother. 'It means not in front of the children. She loves saying that, doesn't she?'

'How do you spell *bonjour*?' asked Holly.

Imogen spelled out the letters and then began to count off her five hellos on her fingers.

'*Guten Tag* is next. That's German,' she boasted.

'And then there's *buon giorno* – that's Italian . . .'

'You're such a show-off,' said Holly bravely. 'And anyway, don't go so fast . . .'

'And you're a pathetic slowcoach,' sniffed Imogen. 'I shan't tell you what they say in Hungary or Czechoslovakia . . .'

'I don't care!' snarled Holly.

'"Don't care was made to care",' retorted Imogen, and she stalked towards the door.

'"Don't care was hung!"' she added ominously as she flung open the door.

And there was their grandmother.

'Girls! Girls!' she cried, seeming not to notice the quarrel. 'Come quickly to the drawing-room. You were making such a noise in here you missed the sleigh bells! Father Christmas is here!'

'Father Christmas!' said Holly breathlessly.

'Father Christmas?' echoed Imogen just as eagerly.

Together the girls rushed past Phoebe, but when they reached the door of the drawing-room they paused and looked at one another.

'Go on!' said Guy from behind them. 'Knock! He won't eat you!'

Imogen knocked.

'Come in!' came a growling kindly old voice.

Holly struggled with the door knob. Imogen helped her.

The room was in darkness except for the huge, blazing fire, and empty but for Father Christmas, sitting in Hereward's favourite chair.

He was holding out a sack.

'Come, children, come and choose a last present from old Father Christmas!' growled the kind old voice.

They crept forward solemnly and dipping their hands into the sack drew out a parcel each.

'Do I get a hug?' said Father Christmas.

The two girls approached him, dropped quick kisses somewhere into his beard and fled from the room.

Outside the door they looked at one another, for the first time as friends.

'It wasn't Granddad . . . was it?' faltered Imogen shyly.

'N-no . . . I don't think so . . .'

On their way home to The School Lodge that evening they ran down the hill hand in hand.

Part Three
Holly and Hugo

9

The refugee

Not long after Christmas the boys had come back to The Priory. When Holly wanted to visit her grandmother she had to make her way shyly down the passages smelling of cabbage and boot polish, among a seething sea of grey flannel, white shirts, crooked ties, wrinkled socks and heavy black shoes.

But now she did not have much time to spend with Phoebe. She went every morning to Miss White's in old Swanstown, close by the duck pond, to a grey stone house with blue paint on the doors and windows. There she sat under Miss White's stern eye, with a host of other small girls in purple uniform, doing reading, writing and arithmetic, and sometimes – just before it was time to go home – a little drawing, painting or sewing.

Kitty walked her there and back, up the steep hill and down again, Holly proudly clinging to the long drawstring of her shoe bag. It was her most precious possession. Kitty had made it for her, even embroidered a large H on it. It contained all the shoes she needed for her new life: indoor shoes and outdoor shoes and plimsolls for drill when they stood in straight lines and did exercises; dancing shoes for dancing class after school on Fridays and shiny patent leather party shoes. She made friends with Patricia, the doctor's daughter, and Priscilla, the vicar's daughter, who had known each other, they boasted, since almost the day they were born. They had been told to be nice to the new girl from Africa and they were nice to her. Holly sat next to them at school, danced with them at dancing class, met them at parties. They were friendly but not real friends. Holly had never yet had a real friend.

At breakfast one March morning, towards the end of that first term, the telephone rang in The School Lodge.

Kitty jumped up and went into the hall to answer it.

'It's for you, Guy! Long distance – it's Miles. He says it's urgent . . .'

'Miles?' Guy dropped his napkin. 'Where is he? What on earth can he want at this hour?'

He hurried out of the room.

'Eat up,' said Kitty to Holly, drumming her fingers on the table.

'Kitty!' called Guy, his voice sharp, excited. 'Come here quickly, darling, will you?'

Alone with her toast fingers and her boiled egg, Holly

heard her father and mother arguing fiercely. Their voices were so loud and angry she could not help hearing almost every word.

'What do you mean?' Kitty was shouting. 'What do you mean, bring out refugee children from Czechoslovakia? It's madness! You don't know what you're getting into! It's nothing to do with us. Your duty is here with your wife and child . . . all very well for Miles! He hasn't got a family. He's mad! Crazy! One day he'll fly too close to the sun . . .'

'He's my brother, Kitty! It's a brave attempt. I'd like to do my little bit. Hell's bells, Kitty, it could be our child's life at stake . . .!'

'But it's not our child! Jews in danger of their lives? Things can't be as bad as that! He must be exaggerating. He's hysterical . . . you're hysterical . . .'

'I'm sorry, Kitty, but I'm going and I must go now – at once . . .'

'All right then! Abandon your wife and child!'

'Kitty, don't be ridiculous! I'll be back in a day or two. Besides, I'm leaving you in the bosom of my family!'

'Huh!'

'Darling, please try to understand. And not a word, eh? Not a word to anyone outside the family. Apparently Miles has talked to our parents and, if all goes according to plan, they are willing to take in a child . . . sponsor one . . . aren't they wonderful?'

51

'Wonderful,' said Kitty sourly.

Holly heard Guy bounding upstairs.

Kitty came back, poured herself tea shakily, clattering the cup against the saucer.

'Where's Daddy going?' said Holly.

'To see Uncle Miles . . .'

'Why?'

'Never you mind. Just hurry up and finish your breakfast.'

Guy came back in his overcoat, his old school scarf tossed round his neck, holding a cricket sweater.

He kissed Holly.

'Goodbye, darling. Back in a day or two. Look after your mother, there's a good girl.'

'Why are you clutching that sweater?' said Kitty, as Guy gingerly kissed the top of her head.

'Miles said to bring warm clothes. Says you get very cold flying . . .'

'Flying?' Holly lunged after the exciting word.

'Ssh!' said Guy, laying a finger to Holly's lips. 'Not a word to anyone, mind. Not a word. Our secret. Word of honour, eh? Word of honour. That's what we used to say at school. Word of honour, understand?'

All the way to school Holly's feet went 'word-of-honour-understand'. Her father and Uncle Miles were doing something dangerous and secret. Something they would do for her if they had to. So why did her mother mind? She longed to ask her, but Kitty wasn't in the mood for talking at the moment.

'Word-of-honour,' Holly breathed, seeing her breath in the bitter March air.

All day long she hugged the secret to herself as she giggled with Patricia and Priscilla, tried to understand long division, struggled to thread her needle and knot her thread, and endlessly changed from outdoor shoes to indoor shoes to plimsolls and dancing shoes.

'Word of honour. Back in a day or two . . .'

Guy's day or two turned into nearly a week.

Holly had long been fast asleep by the time her father and uncle arrived in the middle of the night at The School Lodge with Hugo Altman.

But when she came down for breakfast she noticed the extra place laid at the table.

'There's a little boy in the spare room,' said Kitty. 'Go up and fetch him down for breakfast.'

'You come too,' said Holly.

'No, he's very shy. He'll feel happier with another child.'

'Daddy . . . I'll get Daddy.'

'No, Daddy's resting. He's very tired.'

'Did they . . . did they really go to . . .'

'Czechoslovakia? Yes, they did.'

'And bring back . . .'

'Some little Jewish refugees . . .'

'What's "Jewish refugees"?'

'They're escaping from Hitler. You know about Hitler. Daddy told you about Hitler before we left Africa. He told me he did. He told you: Hitler is a very bad man, a very greedy man who keeps marching into other people's countries . . . that's why Daddy is sure there will be a war . . . sooner or later Hitler has got to be stopped. And he doesn't like Jews. He hates them. He wants to stop them . . .'

'Stop them from what?'

Kitty sighed.

'We-ell,' she said vaguely, yet ominously, 'from everything, really.'

'You mean . . . kill them?' whispered Holly.

'Yes . . . we-ell, that's what people are saying. I don't believe that myself. After all, you can't kill millions of people, can you? But he does seem to want to put them into sort of prison camps away from everyone else . . .'

'But why?' Holly persisted. 'What are Jews? They must just be people like us?'

'Of course they are people, but . . . but . . .'

'But what?'

'They aren't like us. They're . . . different . . .'

'How . . . different?'

'We-ell, we are fair and they are dark . . .'

'But you are dark, Mummy.'

'Yes, but . . . theirs is a different kind of darkness. You'll see. And . . . and they're very clever and good at getting rich . . .'

'Is that bad?'

'No, of course not. It just depends how you do it. And . . . they don't believe in Jesus . . .'

'Oh!' gasped Holly.

Every night she said her prayers to gentle Jesus, meek and mild. How could anybody not believe in Jesus?

'As a matter of fact,' Kitty added, 'you could say the Jews killed Jesus . . .'

'Killed Jesus?'

'Well, whatever else, they certainly helped to make sure he got killed.'

Holly clasped her hands against her chest as she always did when deeply troubled.

At last she said firmly, 'But *he* didn't.'

'Who didn't?' said Kitty impatiently.

'The little boy upstairs. He wasn't there . . .'

'Oh, Holly! It's impossible to explain. It's very complicated. There are so many things. Their ways are not our ways and their God isn't our God. Well, He is and He isn't. Oh, darling, for heaven's sake, just go and fetch the wretched boy down for his breakfast . . .'

'What's his name?'

'Hugo. Hugo Altman.'

'Where are his mother and father?'

'Don't ask me! I don't know. They couldn't come. Miles and Daddy couldn't rescue everyone . . .'

'When will they be coming?'

'Oh, Holly! I don't know! Now be nice to him. He is different from us. He can't help that. You just be very nice to him. Now go on. Go and fetch him, please!'

'Does he know any English?'

'Of course not! He's all that to learn and we will have to help him. German is his language . . .'

'Then what shall I say to him?'

'Oh, I don't know! You'll find something . . . now, go on! Hurry up!'

Holly took as long as she could going up the stairs and lingered outside the door to the spare room. It took her ages to find the courage to knock and when she did there was no answer.

Slowly she turned the knob and opened the door.

The boy was sitting on the bed. He was dressed and he looked as though he'd washed his face and brushed his hair.

Slowly Holly walked to the end of the bed.

'*Guten Tag*, Hugo,' she heard herself say, then, pointing to herself, added, 'I am Holly.'

10
'The Ger-mans have marched into Prague'

Downstairs Hugo took out the envelope his father had given him. He had kept it in his pocket ever since and slept with it under his pillow last night.

Now he handed it to Kitty.

Kitty stared at the foreign, curly handwriting.

'What's this?' she asked.

'He wants you to have it, Mummy,' said Holly.

'I can see that,' snapped Kitty. She stood it on the mantelpiece.

'Tell him I'll give it to your father,' she said.

Holly pointed desperately to the letter and said, 'Father. Father.'

Hugo struggled to understand.

'*Vater*? Father?'

'Yes,' said Holly firmly. 'Father. My father . . .'

'*Gut*,' said Hugo. Mr Nash's brother, he thought.

'Yes,' said Holly. 'Good.'

'Well,' said Kitty. 'Quite the little linguists! What are you waiting for, Holly? Pass Hugo the bread and butter.'

When Guy at last appeared just before lunch she gave him the letter from Hugo's father. Guy studied the envelope.

'It's his name and their address in Prague.' He read out the words underlined beneath Hugo's name and address in his awful German accent: '*An wen es sich bezieht . . .*'

Over lunch, he opened the letter, and studied the flimsy paper for a long time.

'Well,' he admitted at last. 'I can't make head or tail of it, except that there are some more addresses . . . in France, I think . . . Mother will be able to translate it . . . her German is pretty good.'

'It all seems so dramatic,' protested Kitty.

'Not if you'd seen it with your own eyes,' said Guy sombrely. 'I'll never forget that little airport full of those wretched men, weeping women and children. No, my dear, it's not dramatic. It's beyond our comprehension, I grant you, but seeing is believing and those people are terrified, I can tell you . . . I'll pass the letter on to Father and Mother for safekeeping anyway, since if war breaks out – or, I should say when war breaks out – I won't be here.'

'You're still determined to join up, aren't you?' said Kitty.

'Yes, my darling,' said Guy. He kissed her gently on the forehead. 'You know I am . . . more than ever now.'

'I'm proud of you, Guy,' said Kitty, patting his hand affectionately.

Then she turned to the children, as if she had only just remembered they were there.

'Rest time!' she ordered. 'Holly, you can take Hugo up to the nursery. Give him a book or something.'

Up in the nursery Hugo huddled in an armchair large enough for two. He longed to cry, but the tears didn't come. It seemed that ever since he'd got up he'd been listening to grown-ups talking. And although they had been talking in a language he didn't understand, he knew they had been talking about him. Sometimes he had wanted to hit them and say, 'What are you saying? What are you saying? Tell me! Tell me in my language! What's happening? What is going to happen to me?'

And now he had been brought to this room at the top of the house. Holly had pointed her toys out to him and opened a book and put it on his lap: a picture of an elephant with a yellow crown. He stared blindly at Babar, Celeste, Cornelius, the Old Lady, but all he saw were the faces of his mother and father on that last morning in Prague . . .

'*Comeandseethesea!*' Holly begged, pointing to the window. 'The sea! The sea!' She sounded so excited and wanting him to be happy that Hugo got up and went to the window with her. And there he saw water – water as far as the edge of the world. Sea . . . sounds a bit like *See*, Hugo said to himself, *See* . . . a lake . . . could it be a big lake? He knew about lakes. There were many in his own country, high up in the mountains. 'Sea . . . sea . . .' Papa had told him that England was an island . . . what had Mr Nash said in the car last night? *Im Morgen wirst du das Meer sehen* . . . so this was it! This was sea. He looked eagerly at Holly. How to say: *When can we go down there*? *When can we go near the sea*? Holly seemed to understand. 'When Mummy comes,' she said.

And sure enough, when 'rest time' was over, Kitty took the children down to the kiosk on the seafront. She walked them briskly along. Hugo would have liked to take her hand, but noticed that Holly didn't. He wondered why.

While Kitty chose a postcard of Swanstown's ornate pier, Hugo turned again and again to stare at the sea, excited by the steely grey waves crashing on to the sand, then drawing back, leaving a lacy fringe. They went to the Post Office to buy a stamp for Czechoslovakia. *'Don'tdawdle,'* Kitty ordered, as Hugo trailed after her. He was getting a headache from trying to understand the unknown language. It was like being in a fog.

The postmistress had to look up how much a stamp cost to Czechoslovakia.

While she was doing that, Kitty suddenly turned to Hugo and said, slowly and loudly, 'Oh yes! The Germans have marched into Prague. Understand? *The Ger-mans have ma-arched in-to Prague.'*

Somehow Hugo did understand. Something bad had happened in Prague.

'What's Prague?' Holly asked as they hurried along the esplanade.

'The capital of Czechoslovakia,' said Kitty. 'Like London is the capital of England. Where Hugo's family lives.'

At home again, Kitty sat Hugo down at the dining-room table with a new nib in her penholder and the inkwell from Guy's desk resting on a blotter.

'Write,' she commanded, plonking the postcard in front of him and handing him the pen. 'Write to your father and mother.'

Hugo did as he was told.

'Beloved parents,' he wrote. 'I am well. I hope you are well. The plane was an adventure. I have seen the sea. I am by the sea. It is nice. The people are nice. The food is nice. The little girl is nice. *What are the German uniforms like*? I send many kisses. Until we meet again, your Hugo.'

That is what he wrote, but in his head he was saying other things: *When are you coming? Soon, I hope. It is not all nice here. But I do like Holly, the little girl. She is friendly, but her mother is not. She is not even very kind to Holly. She does not kiss her and does not hold her hand. She does not tuck me up at night like you, Mummy. Come soon, please. I miss you, I miss you, I miss you . . .*

As promised, Guy went over to the school with Hugo's letter. He found his parents together in Hereward's study.

'"To Whom It May Concern",' Phoebe translated for them.

61

'Oh!' she bristled. 'How impersonal! How unfriendly. "In the event",' she continued, '"in the event of our not being able to fetch our son, Hugo Altman, in person once the present situation has been resolved, kindly communicate with my sister, Mme Anne Levi, either at her address in Paris or at her holiday residence in Nice. See below".'

She handed the letter to Hereward.

'It's all too dreadful! What do they envisage? What do they fear is going to happen?'

'Oh, Mother,' sighed Guy. 'I didn't understand either until Miles set me right on our way to Prague. The Jews over there have been sitting on a time bomb for years. But I suppose they could not believe that they are hated so much, that the Germans want to get rid of them all. The story is far from over, I fear . . .'

Hereward fingered the letter unhappily. He looked tired and very sad.

Phoebe covered her ears. 'I don't want to hear any more. Put it away, Hereward. Put it away until the day comes when we can tear it up and throw it into the nearest wastepaper basket.'

'Pray God,' Hereward said, 'pray God we'll never need it . . .'

Two weeks later a postcard came for Hugo from his parents. At the bottom his father had written: 'The German uniforms aren't bad, as uniforms go.'

He shut himself in the lavatory to read it before folding the stiff paper messily into four and stuffing it in his pocket.

Then he cried softly, somehow feeling he should not have asked his father what the German uniforms were like, yet knowing that his father understood his curiosity and still loved him as much as he ever had.

All the same, that day he could not eat a thing, except an old sticky sweet Holly fished out of her pocket and gave to him on the stairs at bedtime. He wished he could talk to her, but apart from thank you, he had no words.

11

Hugo's new world

Hugo was taken into the school immediately.

'The sooner he gets the hang of things the better,' said Hereward.

He then sent for his prefects and form monitors and, flanked by Robert Pendleton and Guy, gave them a brief lecture.

'Now,' he began briskly. 'You know all about the new boy, Altman, and how Mr Nash here went with his brother to rescue him – and other children – from . . . er . . . his part of the world where there's . . . er . . . a lot of trouble at the moment.'

'Yes, sir!' said one of the older boys, looking at Guy with admiration.

'Jolly exciting, sir!' said another before he was pulled up short by the severe, sad expression in Guy Nash's eyes.

'Mm,' Hereward went on. 'Sadly, Altman has been parted – for the time being, that is – from his parents. Try to put yourselves in his place, will you? Very far from home. A stranger in a foreign land. A new language to be learned and so on. And yes, another thing . . . Altman is a Jew . . . and that's a tricky subject I won't go into now. I'll keep it simple. He has different beliefs from ours, but, at the end of the day, the same God watches over all His children. I want no teasing, no baiting, no tomfoolery of any kind, and I trust you older chaps to keep an eye on him – at least until he's settled down. I'm sure you can handle this, but if you find you can't I want you to come straight to me. Is that understood? Good. That'll be all.'

'Poor little blighter,' said Robert Pendleton to Hereward when they were alone again.

'Yes,' agreed Hereward. 'I know we've never done it before for any new boy, but perhaps you'd take Altman to his form and introduce him to his master and the other boys?'

'Right you are!' said Robert happily. 'Rules are made to be broken!'

Hugo found that first term very hard. He exhausted himself, watching, watching, listening, listening. Sometimes he wanted to lash out, even kick or bite one of the boys in his desperate frustration at every turn.

On Sundays after tea and before prayers, the boys had to write a letter home. Hugo wrote the same short, stiff, reassuring sentences as he had on his first postcard.

But in his mind he let the true picture flow and spread across page after page of large imaginary sheets of paper:

'*It's awful. It's awful. I don't understand what they're saying. They talk too quickly or too loudly. Then my head aches . . . I can't tell them anything . . . ask them anything . . . properly. They try to help me. They smile at me and point at things . . . the door to the lavatories, where to put my coat and shoes – and which is to be my desk. I follow them about trying to get the hang of things. But I can tell they get fed up with me, because they soon stop smiling and sometimes they even sigh . . . or roll their eyes up and say, "Oh Lord, Altman, oh Lor' . . ."*

'*The food is disgusting and smells and tastes quite different from your food, Mummy. We have something called macaronicheese and custard, every day this custard poured all over stodgy pudding. But even worse is rice pudding where the skin on top is all burnt, but you have to eat it! One day I will be sick, I know I will. At teatime, we eat thick stale bread with Marmite. Ugh! stinging, salty dark brown stuff spread on the butter, only I don't think it is real butter . . . I miss hot chocolate and fresh white rolls with poppy seeds . . . I miss your soup at supper, Mummy, with black bread. And there's no gherkins, no red peppers, no goulash, no Schnitzel. Instead we get watery cabbage stuff, fatty bits of meat swimming in foul brown sauce and horrible hard cheese – mousetrap I heard the boys call it. I am always hungry after the awful meals, I do not know yet how to ask for more and I am afraid they will think I am greedy if I do.*

'*We sleep in a dorm – ten of us. The windows are open even* when it is cold. The blankets are thin. There are no hot radiators or stoves here. Even the light switches are different, and the pillows – not square but long and lumpy. Sometimes the boys have fights with them till Matron comes in and shouts at them.

'But the worst is the bath – it is huge and first thing every morning we all have to plunge into the water – cold – together! I hate it. I hate it. Being naked in front of all the others, the splashing, the laughing, the pushing, the shoving.

'Next worse is chapel. That is their synagogue, but it does not look like the one we go to on our Holy Days. We sing hymns about someone called Jesus. Well, they sing. I don't.

'I watch the boys bait each other and make up again and sometimes I wish they would bait me and make friends again like that.

'When we go to the beach in crocodile, the master always has to make one of them walk with me – and then we're the only ones not chattering.

'Lessons are a bit better, though. Art is still my best and Maths is all right because the numbers are the same and sound quite like German. Geography is all right because the maps are the same, but large bits of them are coloured red to show the British Empire. And I do like Latin because the boys find it just as difficult as I do and I like the Latin master, Mr Pendleton. He is always kind to me like Holly is always kind to me.

'On Saturdays I go to Holly's house and I am to spend the holidays there.

'Holly's grandmother explained this to me. She speaks German!

But she told me she will not always speak it with me as I have got
to learn English. And I have told her I have decided never to speak
German again – I don't want the people here to think I am on
Hitler's side.

  'Holly's mother is giving me grammar lessons. She makes me
learn words I have to write down in a book. I do not think she likes
teaching me. She gets cross when I make mistakes. She does not like
it if I am sad. I am sad because I miss you and I do not get letters
from you. If I got letters from you I could swap the stamps . . . After
the lesson I play with Holly.

'You must talk to him!' Kitty would snap at poor Holly. 'I
can't be expected to do it all! How else will he learn? Talk to
him when you play with him!'

And she would escort them herself, or send them with
Florence, the daily help, to play clock golf or build
sandcastles or look for shells on the beach.

  They liked going with Florence. They liked her simple,
comforting murmurs as she buttoned them up or fed them
sandy Maltesers from the depths of her pockets.

  'They don't have any seaside in Hugo's country,' Holly
informed Florence.

  'Well, then! He can hardly be expected to know how to
build a sandcastle, can he?' said Florence. 'Go on, then!
Show him!' And she would get down on her stiff knees and
help, repeating the words softly as Holly talked Hugo
through: 'That's it! Fill the bucket like this, see! Pat . . . pat

68

the sand down nice and smooth . . . tip out . . . *upside down*, like this, see?'

Up in the nursery Holly read to him about Babar, Zephir and the Old Lady – stories she knew by heart – stabbing at the pictures with a dramatic finger: 'Oh look! Ssnake! Oh! The snake's bitten her! Ohh! Poor Old Lady! Look! Zephir's getting help! She's not going to die!'

With Hugo's box of delicate treasures they built fantasy islands . . . 'That blue material can be the sea . . . this silver chair the *king's throne* . . . let's make a procession of *elephants* . . . *a family of all these cats* . . . these dogs can be guarding those little pixies in case that big brown bear comes out of that forest of palm trees . . .'

Or they played on the rocking horse, where, 'My turn, your turn, my turn', became a frequent refrain, which Hugo enjoyed.

Hugo already loved Holly. He had loved her for saying *Guten Tag* that first morning. Now he loved her for playing with him, for helping him, for never asking any questions. And school was gradually becoming easier as his English got better. The other boys grew friendlier and began to let him join the bands of gangsters, pirates or soldiers with imaginary machine guns which sprang up during break . . .

'I understand the boy has a real gift for drawing and painting,' Hereward told Phoebe one evening. 'Miss Peacock is really impressed – says she even got a smile out of him when she pinned one of his paintings up in the studio . . .'

At last letters began to arrive from his parents, short ones, as cheerful as his were to them.

Slowly, very slowly, Hugo's great raw wounds of loss and loneliness were beginning to heal.

12

A surprise

In the summer holidays Imogen came down to Swanstown.

Phoebe brought her over to The School Lodge to join Holly and Hugo.

'*Guten Tag*, Hugo!' she showed off.

'*Guten Tag*!' Hugo replied happily. '*Sprichst du Deutsch*?'

'What?' said Imogen.

Holly could not help smiling. It seemed Imogen's German was not so good after all.

'I know Prague,' Imogen rattled on. 'How old are you? Are you homesick? There's going to be a war soon, you know. You will stay here a long time . . .'

Hugo stared at her. Holly hoped he didn't understand everything Imogen had said.

Imogen gave up on this dumb boy and turned on Holly.

'If there is a war,' she said triumphantly, '*my* daddy isn't going to fight. He doesn't believe in killing people like *your* daddy . . .'

It was Holly's turn to be struck dumb.

But before she could think of something to say Imogen had moved on.

'You don't have cricket in your country, do you,' she said to Hugo. 'Not even French cricket. We'll play that tomorrow . . .'

'Imo! Imo!' Phoebe broke in. 'Give the poor boy a chance!'

'Can Hugo swim?' Imogen demanded as she and Holly changed in one of the little wooden huts on the beach. She had already chased Hugo into an empty one, yelling after him, 'Boys can't get undressed with girls in this country!'

'I don't know,' said Holly. 'He must have been swimming in the summer term . . .'

'Will he understand if I ask him?'

'I can swim,' was Hugo's answer. 'But not in sea till I come here . . . in my country we have no sea . . . but in . . . in *Schwimmbad* – swim . . . bath?'

'Swimming pool,' Holly said gently.

'In swim pool – I swim . . .'

'Pooh!' said Imogen. 'Anyone can swim in a swimming pool. It's much more difficult in the sea because of the waves . . .'

'Yes,' said Holly defiantly, 'but the sea holds you up more . . .'

'I try again,' said Hugo and, running ahead of the girls, plunged into the water.

Imogen rushed in after him showing off her breaststroke, her head well above water, as even she had never found the courage to put her head underwater.

Holly couldn't help laughing at the sight of her bossy cousin with her head turning this way and that like some small bird as she checked on Hugo and how much further out he had got than her.

She stood nervously at the water's edge until Hugo called, 'Come, Holly! I help you!'

'Yes!' agreed Imogen magnanimously, 'I'll help you . . . we'll both help you!'

Holly waded in slowly.

'Let me get used to it first,' she begged, ducking in up to her neck. 'Daddy taught me this . . .'

And she started to dog paddle.

Imogen burst out laughing, and Hugo grinned.

'You very nice dog!' he said.

'Can you float, Hugo?' challenged Imogen.

'Float?'

'Yes, you know: Swim on your back . . . like this . . .'

'Oh yes . . . *float*,' repeated Hugo, promptly doing so beautifully, then shooting off quite some distance with a powerful thrust of his skier's legs.

'You,' he called to Imogen. 'You? Can you?'

'N-no, not like that,' admitted Imogen '. . . only if someone holds me up in the middle . . .'

'After lunchtime, I help you . . .' Hugo offered.

'After lunch,' corrected Imogen, 'I'm going to teach you French cricket.'

But after lunch Miles came.

It had been a well-kept surprise.

He came striding into The School Lodge, and, like Hugo, Holly fell at once and for ever under his spell. His coppery gold hair gleamed in the sun, and he was beautiful like Baldur the sun god in her favourite book of Norse tales. She noticed that everyone turned towards him because he was quiet. He was like a candleflame, burning but steady. He said nothing at all about his work, or about war, or peace. He came and he went, and when he was with them he was really with them, and everyone felt the better for his presence.

'Hello, Hugo,' he said quietly. 'We meet again.' His gaze, searching yet gentle, would often return to Hugo when Hugo was not looking.

He hugged Holly and called her his mystery niece from faraway lands, and swung Imogen high off her feet.

'I can only stay for two days,' he said, 'so let's make the most of it! This afternoon we will go to the fair and this evening, I thought we might take a boat out . . . might put out a line for mackerel . . . has anyone beaten me to it?' he added, looking at Hugo.

'Beaten you to what?' asked Imogen.

'Has anyone taken Hugo out on the water?'

Everyone looked mildly ashamed.

'I have been in the sea,' said Hugo, 'but not yet on it!'

Miles smiled.

'Good,' he said. 'Well, how about going out to sea?'

Hugo was overwhelmed. To go in a boat with Mr Nash. Maybe to be allowed to learn to row . . .

'Y-Yes,' he managed. 'Yes. Please. I like that very much. When?'

'This evening,' said Miles. '*Am Abend* . . .'

All that hot afternoon the three children rode the merry-go-round with Miles and bumped in bumper cars with Miles, and gorged themselves on Knickerbocker Glories. As the sun began to sink, they climbed unsteadily into a rocking rowing-boat, and, with a helping hand, played out string and hooks for mackerel. And later Hugo's wish came true: they each took a turn at the oars while Miles sang them sea shanties.

For the first time since he had left home, Hugo felt really happy.

That night the children slept at once and slept long and deeply, as if still in the presence of Miles in that boat.

They woke up to another cloudless summer's day, but Miles was gone.

Hugo looked as if he might be going to cry.

Holly did cry.

For once Imogen came to the rescue.

'Don't forget last night he did say "*Au revoir*". You remember what that means, Holly. I told you . . . It's "*Auf Wiedersehen*" in French, Hugo . . . Goodbye till we see each other again.'

13

War breaks out

The day the war broke out Holly and Hugo were in Scotland.

Guy had suddenly taken it into his head to go grouse shooting.

He swept Kitty and the children away to a small hotel near heathery moors where he shot birds all day and ate them every night.

He and Kitty would have liked to have left Hugo behind in Swanstown. But his mother had fixed him with a beady eye and said, 'But who with, poor boy?'

It was a peaceful, beautiful Sunday morning. The sky was pure blue, the sun warm, the village quiet, the smell of roast dinners floating on the air, the one street empty with most people at church, little knowing their bells had just rung for the last time for many years.

Holly and Hugo had been on the way back to the hotel from a walk with Kitty. They had been in the cool, green woods where they had found a fairy ring of toadstools beneath the ancient beech trees.

'Don't touch them!' Kitty had said. 'They're poisonous . . . but go on then! Make a wish! But don't tell anyone what it is if you want it to come true!'

Holly stepped into the magic circle. What to wish for?

When she last cut the first slice of her birthday cake she had wished for what she called 'a forever-friend'. And now, standing in the fairy ring she suddenly realised her wish had come true. She had Hugo. 'I will use my wish for him,' she said to herself. She closed her eyes for a while and bent her head. Then, looking up into the lovely lacy patterns of the trees she wished that soon her friend would see his mother and father again.

'A wish,' she said to Hugo, as she stepped carefully over the toadstools. 'I make a wish, for you . . . but it's a secret.'

She put a finger to her lips. 'Secret,' she repeated. 'Good wish. Can't tell you . . .'

Hugo smiled at her. 'We do this too,' he told her. 'Now, *my turn!*'

And he stepped into the ring and made his good wish.

They were walking back to the hotel up the village street when suddenly the air was filled with a terrifying wailing, like some new, ugly music. On and on it went in an ever-louder yowling spiral as if an unknown wild beast was coming to get them out of the dark wood.

Kitty stopped and looked round and up. Her lips were

moving but the noise was so deafening Holly couldn't hear what she was saying.

At last with a dreadful sliding moan, as if the creature had exhausted its own pain, the sound stopped.

'That was an air-raid siren,' gasped Kitty into the sudden, shocking silence. 'Oh, my God! What's happened?'

As if in answer, windows flew up, doors flew open and there were people everywhere yelling, 'Better get indoors quickly! War's been declared . . .!'

Kitty's mouth fell open. 'Oh no!' she cried out. Then she grabbed Holly's hand and began running so fast that Hugo could hardly keep up.

Suddenly there was Guy, running towards them up the street.

'Germany has invaded Poland! War's been declared!' he called out to them. 'The Prime Minister has just spoken on the wireless . . .'

He and Kitty joined the people crowded round the wireless in the hotel, while the children hovered in the doorway. Suddenly all the men rushed outside and looked up anxiously into the sky.

Holly tugged at her mother's hand. 'What are they doing?' she asked fearfully.

'Looking for aeroplanes,' said Kitty. 'They think there might be an air raid already on Glasgow . . .' She was looking at all the excited men rather scornfully, and smiled at Holly when a flock of birds flew over their heads: swallows leaving early.

'See, Holly,' she said. 'Just birds . . .'

In the few days that followed, before their swift return to Swanstown, Holly lived her own nightmare. For the first time she wished Hugo wasn't there, always at Kitty's elbow asking questions to which she did not know the answers.

'Is killing in my country? Where will be my mother and father now?'

'How many times do I have to tell you, Hugo,' Kitty would snap. 'I don't know. I don't know . . .'

Somehow Holly never had a chance to tell her mother of her own fears.

The worst one was the dark metal bird – the plane from a nearby aerodrome, – a 'Spitfire' her father had told her – which took to flying over the hotel.

How she dreaded the sound of its low growly throb coming steadily closer and closer, growing louder and louder, shutting out the pure blue sky as it flew low over the hotel, almost touching the roof itself. The stabbing fear she felt now was the same as when she'd heard the foghorns sobbing as the great ship bringing her from Africa had crept towards England.

'It's only a plane,' Guy would say. 'It's high time you stopped being such a scaredy-cat . . .'

'But I always have been,' Holly confided to Hugo when they were alone again. 'I hate loud noises . . . bangs . . . balloons popping . . . crackers at Christmas. Whenever we have fireworks I always run indoors and hide in the curtains

. . . and it always makes Daddy cross . . . but this plane is the worst thing I have ever been afraid of . . .'

'I am afraid also,' Hugo said, 'I am afraid if one time it will not be a Spitfire, but a German plane – a *Messerschmitt* – who will . . . will . . . kill us.'

With Hugo at her side, Holly would cower in the hotel garden as the plane flew lower, ever lower, casting its shadow over them as they crouched among the bright tall autumn flowers. She cowered, but could not tear her eyes away from the Spitfire. Waggling its wings playfully as it began to swoop upward and away, she could see the waving hand of the pilot, and his laughing face, enjoying his game. She knew who he was, of course: Uncle Tony she was allowed to call him. He was a friend of her parents, and often came into the hotel with the other pilots to share her father's grouse.

Even so she wanted to run, run into the house and hide herself in Kitty's skirts.

But she didn't; couldn't.

Her father might be watching her, even blocking the doorway to halt any flight.

He'd taken to doing this ever since the first time she'd come running, screaming, her hands over her ears, failing to block out the sound she found so fearful: the nearness of it, the unknownness of it. She'd come slap up against his legs at the door with Hugo close behind her.

'Get back out there at once, both of you!' he'd shouted.

Then in a gentler voice, 'There's a war on and you're just going to have to get used to the planes, and God alone knows what else . . .'

He'd given Holly a firm shove and gone on standing there, cutting off her escape, watching her creep, snail-like, with Hugo in tow, back into the garden.

Holly had never known her father so stern. What had happened to the kind man who read to her at bedtime? Who crawled about with the green waste-paper basket on his head, pretending to be a crocodile?

'He's only trying to help you,' Kitty had said when at last she'd been able to fling herself, sobbing, into her arms. 'We've all got to be brave now . . . you too, Holly. You've got to be a good, brave girl because soon Daddy will be going away to join the Army . . .'

'But who will look after us?' cried Holly.

'Grandmamma and Granddad, of course,' said Kitty. 'We're going back to Swanstown.'

Holly wiped her eyes and sighed with relief.

If they were going back to Swanstown everything would be all right.

Oh yes, she thought happily, as they whizzed down towards England a few days later on an express train called *The Flying Scotsman*, everything will be all right now.

14

Invasion expected

When Phoebe and Hereward met them at the station they hugged them all as much, if not more, than they usually did. They looked worried and sad.

The day was cold and wet. The white cliffs looked dull and the sea was as grey as the sky. As they drove along with the car windows all steamed up, Holly and Hugo caught mystifying snatches of the grown-ups' conversation.

'Don't know how much longer I'll be allowed to keep the car,' Hereward said. 'They're talking of petrol rationing and of evacuating the South Coast . . . invasion expected . . . the beach will be mined . . .'

'I've had black-out curtains put up for you, Kitty dear,' said Phoebe.

'The Army needs all the large buildings it can get . . . they may even requisition the school . . . we may have to move to somewhere safer . . .'

Holly and Hugo looked at one another – so many new

words neither of them understood. They did not dare to interrupt and ask any questions.

But for a while everything went on in the same way: the sun soon came out again, the air was crisp and the sky such a deep blue that the calm sea looked like a sparkling sapphire.

On Saturdays Holly and Hugo were still allowed to go down to the beach where they ran along the water's edge, hunting for shells, or took their shrimp nets to the rock pools.

Soon they were both back at school. The leaves turned red and yellow and early frost made the spider-webs glitter. The chestnut trees dropped their spiky treasure and Hugo collected conkers with the other boys. He made friends with a rather short-sighted boy called Browning.

'You're really good at finding them,' Browning said one afternoon when they were on a walk in the woods near Swanstown. 'Do you do this in your country?'

'No,' said Hugo. 'But I like to look at different colours because I like to paint and my eye quickly sees them, the green – in among the brown and yellow leaves.'

'Good!' said Browning. 'Will you help me find the biggest and the best?'

'Oh yes!' cried Hugo.

'Then I'll show you how we string them and then we'll have a conker fight with some of the others!'

'And we win?' asked Hugo eagerly.

'We'll have a jolly good try!' agreed Browning.

On the way home in the bright autumn afternoons Holly could smell bonfire smoke. The world still seemed lovely and peaceful.

No planes flew overhead in Swanstown and no air-raid sirens wailed. Holly heard the grown-ups say it was a phoney war. She thought they sounded rather disappointed. But she hoped it had all been a dream and a mistake. There would be no war. Perhaps she wouldn't have to learn to be a 'big, brave girl' after all.

But then her father went away to join up. When he came home again from time to time on leave, he was wearing a soldier's uniform: khaki, it was called. Holly did not think it was a pretty colour, neither green, nor yellow, but rather like the cowpats she used to see in Africa.

Her mother always let her stay up even long past her bedtime to wait for his arrival. Oh, she was so pleased to see him! She didn't even mind the prickle of his new moustache when he kissed her. But his leave always went very quickly and Holly wept bitterly when he left.

Miles never came. He had joined the Navy and disappeared to sea.

One day, suddenly, the beach was out of bounds, shrouded in coils of barbed wire. Ugly, grey, concrete gun emplacements appeared on the cliffs.

Gas masks were tried on. Holly hated the rubbery smell and the tight fit which pulled on her hair every bit as much as a hair brush. She hated the feeling that she could not breathe.

'Don't fuss!' she was told. 'You must carry it with you wherever you go. It could save your life!'

Holly quickly got used to slinging her gas mask in its cardboard box over her shoulder whenever she went out.

Imogen and her parents joined the family for Christmas. Only Miles was missing. 'He's doing such brave work,' Phoebe explained to the children. 'Sailing his ship,' she went on in the loud voice she always used when talking to Hugo. 'Sailing in convoy across the Atlantic, helping families to get their children to safety in Canada and America!'

There was a lovely tree as usual and turkey as usual, and Christmas pudding with real silver threepenny bits in it, and crackers which frightened Holly, as usual. The fruit bowl was full of juicy oranges and ripe bananas. Little did any of them know they would be the last ones they saw or ate for six long years.

After dinner, Father Christmas himself arrived at the front door, his breath like puffs of steam in the frosty air.

The three children went in one by one to visit him in the sitting-room mysteriously lit by firelight and candlelight.

Hugo was happy with a box of paints and brushes. It turned out he was an expert at cracking nuts, and a queue soon formed to await his offerings. He even joined in helping with the huge jigsaw puzzle which was Phoebe's present from Father Christmas.

But when their grandmother called to Holly and Imogen to join them, Imogen suddenly exploded.

'I don't believe in Father Christmas any more,' she announced fiercely. 'There's no such person. Father Christmas is for babies. Anyway that was Granddad in there, wasn't it, Holly?' And she glared at Holly, at Hugo and all the grown-ups. 'Go on! Say so! You know it was, really . . .'

When Holly moved closer to Phoebe and said nothing, Imogen went on like a train with no brakes, running away with itself down a steep hill. 'I don't believe in any of the things you all believe in! If everyone said they wouldn't fight like my daddy has, then there wouldn't be any wars, would there? And . . . and . . . and Hugo wouldn't have to be here . . . he'd be at home with his own mummy and daddy, and my daddy would be here with me instead of working in a place full of mad people . . . You didn't know that, did you, Holly? He's been sent to work in a lunatic asylum, because if he'd refused he would have had to go to prison.'

'Imogen! Imogen!' said Connie angrily.

There was a great silence until Phoebe turned to Imogen and said quietly, 'We're all very proud of your father, darling. Proud of him for sticking to his beliefs . . .'

'Well,' Imogen said, almost shouting, 'I don't care what

86

you think! I just don't believe in anything any more . . .'

Then she burst into tears and ran from the room, followed by her mother.

Phoebe turned to Hugo and Holly, trying to smile.

'Shall we get on with the puzzle?'

As the two children leaned over the jigsaw, Holly asked, 'Hugo, in Prague is there Father Christmas?'

'Yes,' said Hugo, 'but he comes in the street and goes by fast . . . he sits in a . . . a . . .'

'Sleigh?' suggested Phoebe. 'With horses? Bells!'

'*Ja!* Yes!' said Hugo. 'But he does not come in the houses . . .'

'Perhaps that is a better way,' said Phoebe sadly. 'And now, children! Come with me! Let's take old Imo some of that delicious Christmas cake. Holly, you shall cut her a nice big slice with plenty of icing, plenty of marzipan!'

'Marzipan!' breathed Hugo. 'Now that I like!'

'Then you shall have some, too,' said Phoebe.

15
The little brother

Soon after Christmas Guy left again, this time for India. He hugged Holly tightly against his scratchy uniform.

'Look after your mother, eh, Holly? Look after her.'

When he had gone Kitty sent Hugo and Holly up to the nursery, and shut herself away in her room.

The sea was flat and dark. Holly wished Phoebe would come, but she did not. She would have liked to sit on her knee and play with her rings.

She would have liked even more for her mother to come so they could comfort one another.

'You are sad,' said Hugo. 'Why does not your mother come?'

'Because . . . because,' Holly hesitated, 'because of my little brother. He died, you see, when I was being born . . . and . . . and . . . sometimes I think Mummy thinks it was my fault. He got an illness, a brain fever it was called . . . and . . . it was when Daddy was taking Mummy to the hospital a long way from the farm . . . a neighbour was looking after him . . . Timothy he was called . . . but he died even before the doctor came . . . and I am sure if Mummy had been there she would have noticed and got the doctor at once and he would have got better. And then I would have had someone to play with and Mummy would have been so happy and cuddled us both and kissed us often.'

'That is very sad,' said Hugo. 'I am sorry. But it was not your fault. I wish my mother was here. She would hug you and you would feel better. Did you like to live in Africa?'

'Yes,' sighed Holly. 'It was so hot I had to wear a hat and I could take my shoes off and the red earth was warm and the flowers all bright. The sky was always so blue except at night when it was so black and the stars looked like diamonds . . .'

'Diamonds?' said Hugo.

'Yes, you know,' said Holly. 'Those bright stones in Grandmamma's rings . . . the stars glittered like they do. And I did not go to school like we do here. I had a special teacher of my own, a governess, Miss Webster she was called . . . and the neighbours' children came to our farm for lessons with me. We had them in a dear little round house . . . a *rondavel* – Daddy told me it was called – with a roof made of grass . . .'

'Was she a nice teacher?' asked Hugo.

'Oh yes,' said Holly. 'She cried when we left. She was gentle and sad . . .'

'Why?' asked Hugo.

'Because someone she loved very much got killed in the last war . . .'

'There was another war?' said Hugo in horror.

'Oh yes,' said Holly. 'Miss Webster told us all about it. It was called The Great War. It was supposed to be the war to end all wars . . .'

'Well, it didn't, did it?' said Hugo angrily.

'No,' agreed Holly. 'Even though millions of men died, *"Among the mud and poppies of Flanders"*, she said as if it was a poem . . . she often seemed to forget us when she was talking about that war. I expect she was thinking of that man she loved, but her being sad never made her cross like Mummy gets cross with me, especially if I am ill . . .'

'My mother gives me chicken soup when I am ill,' said Hugo proudly.

'Does she?' said Holly.

'And puts cool stuff on my head when I am hot . . .'

'You lucky thing,' sighed Holly.

Hugo fished around in his pocket and brought out a huge, very shiny conker.

'You have this,' he said. 'It is my best . . . I saved it . . . I would not let Browning put the skew– ?'

'Skewer?' suggested Holly.

'Yes, the skewer through it. I did not want it to be spoiled on a string . . . it was too beautiful . . . you have it now . . .'

'Thank you,' whispered Holly, treasuring the conker in

the hollow of her hand. 'Would you like to play *Snakes and Ladders* now?'

In the spring the Army took over The Priory. Swanstown became a restricted area, and certainly no longer a safe place for children.

The Germans had invaded Norway and Denmark. It was only a matter of time before they swept through Holland, Belgium and France. And then, it was believed, it would be England's turn.

One morning Hereward drew Holly and Hugo to the great windows of his study and pointed to the empty sea.

'We can't stay, you see,' he said. 'It isn't safe . . . they will come, and when they come, they will come from there. But we will not close down the school. We must keep our own small flag flying somehow.'

For months Hereward had been looking for a safer place for the school, and for his family. And now Lord Marlowe, an old friend, had come to the rescue. He offered Hereward the use of a very large house for the school and a small house nearby for Kitty and Holly: his entire country estate, in fact, in the beech woods of Buckinghamshire, far from the sea.

And none too soon, for not long after they had all left Swanstown a bomb fell on the school.

16
Marlowes

They came to Marlowes in the lovely April dusk, Holly and Hugo squeezed with Kitty into the back of Hereward's car. They were all tired and hungry after a long day's drive, but excited and eager for a first glimpse of their new home.

They came through open gates up the back drive. On one side there was a paddock without horses and beyond that a huge wood. On the other side was a high wall.

'Kitchen garden in there,' said Phoebe. 'Full of vegetables and fruit!'

They drove past the kitchen garden to the back door of a very large rosebrick house.

'That must be the butler's house,' said Kitty, pointing across the yard to a smaller house crowned with tall thin chimney pots and a white wooden clock tower sitting in the middle of the roof.

'That's where we're going to live, Holly!'

'And Daddy?' said Holly.

'Of course Daddy too,' said Kitty, 'whenever he's on leave.'

'And what about Hugo?'

'He'll be at school, silly, but with us in the holidays as he always is.'

Holly peered sleepily at the butler's house. She thought it looked satisfying in the way a doll's house is satisfying. The top half sat neatly on the bottom half, with all the windows matching above and below.

'We're all going to have such fun!' cried Phoebe, climbing stiffly out of the car. 'Such fun exploring and settling in. The grounds are splendid! Just you wait till morning!'

Wide paths edged the angles of the huge house towering in the dusk, beckoning to unknown worlds. In the distance water gleamed on a lake. Huge trees loomed far away across smooth lawns.

At the back door an old woman met them. She handed Phoebe hundreds of keys, then wobbled away on a bicycle.

They had scrambled eggs on toast at the huge scrubbed table in the cavernous kitchen, where copper pans brought their own warm light to the dim light bulbs and the windows were shrouded in blackout material.

Phoebe, at the head of the table in a high-backed chair, smiled on Holly and Hugo. 'Sleepy heads, all of us! Tonight Hugo can christen a dormitory and Holly and Mummy can share a bedroom.'

'Let's have a quick look round, shall we?' murmured Hereward, puffing tranquilly on his pipe.

He led the way down cold stone passages, which would soon smell of cabbage and shoe polish, and pushed through a door softly covered in thick green baize. It was a heavy door designed to put silence between the lives of servants and masters.

On the far side they stepped on to muffling carpets. The walls gleamed white. Fine furniture shone with beeswax and elbow-grease. Ancestors, trapped in gilt frames, worshipped by dogs, children gambolling at their feet, stared haughtily down at them. Over a massive oak door at the foot of the great staircase there was a bronze plaque stating, *'By right and might let Marlowes hold what Marlowes held.'*

Phoebe clasped her hands reverently in front of it. 'The family motto,' she breathed.

At the top of the wide staircase there was a huge landing with many doors opening on to it.

'Here we are, Hugo!' cried Phoebe in that too-loud voice she always used for him, and she flung open a door on to a large bedroom which had been hastily filled with iron bedsteads, each with a lumpy mattress, a pillow and one thin blanket. 'Beds aren't made up yet, but you can snuggle up somehow.'

The sight of Hugo stepping alone into the empty shadowy room troubled Holly.

Phoebe pushed past her and, gathering blankets from several beds, their frames like prison bars, she thrust them at Hugo.

'Here,' she said kindly, 'you can make yourself a cosy nest.'

Hugo looked at Holly desperately.

'You will leave the landing light on, won't you, Grandmamma?' she begged.

Kitty made noises about blackout regulations, but Phoebe just twitched the ample long velvet curtains tighter and said, 'Of course, darling . . . and I'll leave the door open too!'

Holly could have kissed her.

'Goodnight, Hugo!' Phoebe almost shouted. 'Off to beddy-byes!'

'Goodnight, Mrs Nash,' whispered Hugo.

And then Kitty was tugging Holly across the landing away from Hugo's great eyes staring after them, clutching blankets to his chest.

'And you girls can sleep here in The Red Room!' said Phoebe, her hand on a crystal door knob. 'I remember when Lady Marlowe showed us over. Oh! So interesting! Ribbentrop slept here!'

'Ribbentrop?' Kitty said wearily.

'Yes, dear. You know, the German Ambassador! Slept here only a year or two ago!' Phoebe lowered her voice and added, 'A nasty piece of work, by all accounts.'

She flung the door of the historic bedroom open.

'Look! Red carpet. Red walls covered in silk! Yes, silk, Kitty, silk! Red curtains. Velvet! Red counterpane.'

'But there's only the one bed!' protested Kitty.

'But, dearie, it's enormous! Room for seven dwarfs in there! Put the bolster down between you and tomorrow we'll settle you into your own house . . . And now I must go and settle Hereward and me! We're through there in Lord and Lady Marlowe's suite . . . Very grand! I'll show you in the morning!'

Holly knelt on the enormous bed and traced the picture on the headboard. It felt soft and silky under her finger.

There were little brown rabbits with white bobtails and an apple tree full of flowers and fruit. There was a lovely lady in a blue and gold dress standing in the opening of what looked like a little blue tent. A yellow lion was holding open one side of the tent. A kneeling white unicorn was holding open the other. Above her head were words. Holly traced them with a finger and spelt them out to her mother. '*M-o-n s-e-u-l d-e-s-i-r*. What does that mean?'

'That's French,' yawned Kitty. '*Mon seul désir*. It means, "My one desire".'

'What's desire?'

'Wishing . . . wanting . . . wanting very much . . .'

Kitty climbed into bed, turned out the light.

'Oh, I know what that is!' said Holly happily, sliding down on the other side of the bolster. 'And my one wish . . .'

'Yes, well, my one wish,' Kitty interrupted, 'is to go to sleep.'

'. . . is the same one I made in that fairy ring . . . for Hugo to see his mummy and daddy again soon . . .'

'Ssh!' snapped Kitty. 'You shouldn't have told me! Now it won't come true!'

'Oh I forgot!' cried Holly, horrified at what she'd done.

'Oh, never mind!' said Kitty. 'That's probably only an old wives' tale. The whole thing is a lot of superstitious nonsense anyway. Now, for heaven's sake, go to sleep!'

But Holly lay there worrying. What if it wasn't an old wives' tale? What if it wasn't super . . . super . . . something nonsense? Would it be her fault if it didn't come true?

She turned her face towards the open door. The faint light joined her to Hugo, who was already fast asleep in his nest of scratchy blankets.

17

Out of bounds

'The duck pond is out of bounds,' said Kitty next morning.
'The dairy is out of bounds, the kitchen garden is out of
bounds and the air-raid shelter is out of bounds. Otherwise
you've got the run of the place, so for heaven's sake go out
and play . . .'

She was surrounded by tea chests, unpacking, trying to
make the butler's house her own house.

So Holly and Hugo went out along the cinder path.

'What is out of bounds?' said Hugo.

'Places where we must not go or they will be cross,' said
Holly.

'What is air-raid shelter?'

'I don't know,' said Holly.

'We will look?'

'Yes,' said Holly. 'We will look.'

'What is duck pond?'

'Water. Dangerous. They think we might fall in . . . look!

There it is.' Holly pointed to a brown circle of water. 'That's the pond and here come the ducks.'

A drake and his drab mate waddled up the reedbank, and in their little rippling wake the children saw fragmented reflections of their new world – huge dark trees, half-open iron gates and, near to them, a little round thatched house.

'Let's go and see what that little house is,' said Holly.

Together they pushed at the door of the little round house with its straw roof.

'It's like the one in Africa I told you about!' Holly said to Hugo. 'The *rondavel* where I had my school lessons!'

The round room, damp and cold underfoot, offered the children its long memories of milkiness in all its stages of sweetness and sourness, of butter and cream.

'This must be the dairy,' Holly announced.

'Dairy,' murmured Hugo. 'D-a-i-r-y,' rolling the new word round his tongue.

And Holly knew that at that moment Hugo was happy. And she was happy.

They were together.

'We are out of bounds?' asked Hugo with a smile.

'Yes,' said Holly happily.

'We go on?'

'Yes,' Holly agreed.

'Good!' said Hugo.

And he grinned pure mischief. Now he led the way until they came to a great green field scattered with khaki cowpats and pale yellow flowers that smelled sweeter than the sweetest honey.

They wandered there a long time.

The flowers stood upright, several to a stem on sturdy stalks. Holly began to pick them. Hugo did too. At last he held up a large bunch.

'You give to your mother?' he said.

'Yes.'

'And I give to your . . . grandmother!' Hugo brought out the word triumphantly and repeated it to himself, relishing the word as if it were a sweet.

'What is that?'

He was pointing across the field to a long, grassy mound. It did not look natural. It was symmetrical, man-made.

'I bet that's the air-raid shelter,' said Holly. 'Come on. Let's go and have a look.'

She began to run.

'Out of bounds!' chanted Hugo behind her.

There were pasty grey steps going down into the mound. The steps were covered with last winter's soggy leaves. The door at the bottom was metal and already rusting.

Their defiant feeling of disobedience carried them along.

They crept down the slippery steps and pushed the door open. Benches ran along each side. Pools of water lay on the floor. The place smelled of dank concrete. It was also very cold. It did not feel like a shelter, more like a prison.

They clutched the flowers, crushing the petals between

their fingers. And then Hugo and Holly parted from each other into separate terror.

For Hugo the cold and dark took him towards that other field where he had been torn from his parents.

For Holly a fierce desire overtook her for flight, for sun, sky and earth, flowers, the smell of the sea and warm arms to hold her.

They fled and, stumbling across the fields, slipping in the cowpats, they got lost.

Holly began to cry, but Hugo kept saying, 'Find the grandmother. Find the grandmother . . .'

They came out at last on to an avenue crunchy with gravel and lined with spiky firs, with dark woods in the distance.

The duck pond and the dairy were nowhere to be seen. In their place stood a white stone pond where white lions lay, heads uplifted, craving drink from a fountain which was empty. Beyond lay, not the doll's house where Kitty was making a home, but a different side of the big house they had come to last night, with a large door, flanked by pillars.

This door now opened and out came Phoebe, carrying a flower basket.

'There you are, darlings!' she called, beaming so much her cheeks seemed to ride up. 'Exploring? Me too. I was just going to look for some lilac. Ooh! What have you got there? Cowslips! Lovely, lovely cowslips! Mmm! What a scent!'

And she breathed deeply into the flowers, at the same time looking at the children.

Flowers crushed, she said to herself. Children breathless, trembly, sweaty, shoes covered in dung. They've frightened themselves silly.

'You're both very pale,' she said. 'Where have you been? What is it? Were you lost? Well, never mind! Now you're found! See! This is the front of Marlowes and your house, Holly, is at the back. But where have you been to get so lost?'

'In the fields,' mumbled Holly.

'Out of bounds! Now, you know that's very naughty, Holly. And leading Hugo into mischief! Your mother would be very cross. What frightened you?'

'We found this horrid place . . . down some steps.' Holly faltered.

'Air-raid shelter!' trembled Hugo.

Phoebe shivered.

'Oh, you naughty children! But don't think about it any more and don't ever go there again by yourselves. God willing, we'll never need that beastly old shelter! Now come along with me and I'll show you the summer house!'

She led them to a little white wooden house set down on the lawn which looked like a velvety carpet after the bumpy wildness of the fields.

Phoebe sank back into the hammock and set it swinging.

'See!' she cried, fanning herself the while with a large

leaf fan from India or Africa. 'You can turn the house any way you like, so that you are always, always sitting in the sun and out of the wind. Go on, push it! Help her, Hugo! Yes, that's it! Well done!'

The children pushed and the house moved smoothly on tiny wheels on a circular track.

'You can come and play here any time, and if you're very good I will read to you here.'

She marched them down avenues bordered with huge old trees. 'See! Cedars of Lebanon! We're going to put up climbing ropes! The boys will be pleased! And look at all those bluebells under the copper beeches!'

Phoebe was pointing to the same dark woods which a moment ago had seemed so sinister.

'And isn't the fountain lovely?' she said, patting one of the lions. 'Pity the water's turned off. Rationing, of course.'

She heaved them one by one on to the lions' backs. '*Löwen, nicht wahr*, Hugo? *Löwen!*' she shouted. 'Lions!'

'Yes, Mrs Nash, lions!' Hugo repeated obediently.

'And now!' cried Phoebe. 'Come and see the rose garden! Imagine! A special garden just for roses! And they'll be out in a few weeks!'

She led them towards the huge iron gates Holly had seen reflected in the duck pond's rippling water. They swung open at Phoebe's regal touch.

The garden was walled, and patterned with diamond-shaped beds full of dark shiny leaves, red thorns and secret buds. There was a sundial and a stone birdbath and at the far end, a pavilion reached by shallow steps.

'You can come and play here too,' said Phoebe, 'as long as you don't pick the roses.'

She sank on to a wide stone bench and put her face up to the sun.

'Come!' she said to Holly and Hugo, drawing them one each side of her beneath her cape like a hen with two chicks. 'Let's all sit down for a minute and then I'll show you the way home before it rains. See that little cloud up there! Oh well, April showers! Perhaps there'll be a rainbow later. Let's just sit here a minute and enjoy the quiet . . .'

Holly and Hugo leaned with relief against Phoebe's warmth.

Hugo smiled at Holly across the grandmother's fullness and a thrush began to sing.

18

Fight the good fight

A cricket pitch was hastily mown in the paddock. Boys, who had just parted from tearful mothers and fathers in uniform, arrived for the new term hung with gas masks. Holly watched Hugo cross the backyard from the butler's house and vanish through the back door of Marlowes which had become The Priory School for the duration.

'What's for the duration?' asked Holly.

'For as long as the war lasts,' said Kitty.

Holly stared and stared after Hugo, willing him to look back.

If Hugo didn't look back, she couldn't wave. His shoulders drooped under the grey shirt. His baggy shorts drooped to his knees. He seemed to be dragging his feet, but then the stout black shoes were heavy.

Holly was now willing and willing Hugo to look back; Hugo was willing and willing himself not to look back.

'I do hope Mr Pendleton doesn't throw chalk at Hugo in the Latin lessons,' Holly sighed.

Kitty began to turn away. Holly wondered why she hadn't kissed Hugo goodbye as Grandmamma had earlier? She'd watched her mother sulkily stitch his garters tighter to his skinny legs, so his grey socks wouldn't wrinkle, or, worse still, fall down.

'Who says Mr Pendleton throws chalk at the boys?' Kitty asked irritably.

'Daddy and Uncle Miles. They told me once that his aim was deadly, quite deadly and they told me how Mr Pendleton was wounded in the Great War and he was always grumpy with the pain. That's why he throws chalk at the boys. Mummy, you don't think he's still in pain, do you? It's a long time since that war. Oh, you don't think he will throw chalk at Hugo, do you?'

'Why should he be treated any differently from the other boys?' said Kitty. 'Just because he's a refugee. The other boys will like him less if he's treated differently from them. And you mustn't treat him like a long-lost playmate during term-time, Holly. You don't want him being called a cissy, do you? That's a man's world in there . . .'

Her voice softened when she saw Holly's sad little face.

'But anyway, darling, you'll still see him at school prayers . . .'

And she did. She could just see the back of his head in the grey crowd of boys she and her mother joined in the Marlowes ballroom at the end of each day.

She felt so sorry for Hugo, his head bent low over the

hymn book, pretending to sing while all the other boys sang with their heads up, their mouths wide open like little birds. They knew all the words, all the tunes. They were at home on the old oak floorboards of Marlowes, in the county of Buckinghamshire, England, Great Britain, the Empire, Europe, the World, the Universe.

On the first evening of the summer term, they sang *Fight the Good Fight*.

It was Hereward's favourite hymn and all through the war they were to sing it often.

They sang it the day Holly's father arrived from France, which had now been completely overrun and occupied by the Germans.

Thin, pale, trembling, Guy drew Kitty and Holly to him with tears in his eyes. Kissing them again and again, he clung to them as if he would never let them go. Then, Holly watched horrified as her once strong father clutched at the banisters and, leaning shakily against Kitty, went straight upstairs to bed.

'Is Daddy ill?' asked Holly when Kitty came downstairs again.

'No,' she said, 'he's exhausted and suffering from shock. He's had a terrible time . . . seen terrible things . . .'

Kitty paused, but could not stop herself from continuing angrily.

'Madness, really. Madness . . . or a miracle. It must have looked quite hopeless . . . he . . . he . . . they could have all been killed or captured! He went over the English Channel with all the other soldiers to try and chase the Germans out of France. But they were completely outnumbered and had to flee for their lives . . . and they were not the only ones . . . the roads were choked with all the poor French people trying to get away to safety, pushing prams, dragging cartloads of furniture and food . . . and rich people with chauffeurs tooting their horns to try and clear a way through. Old people, children, babies, dogs, horses, everyone running for cover whenever the German planes flew over, dive-bombing them, flying in really low; firing at them with machine-guns . . . not caring how many they killed . . . and he saw French soldiers just sitting by the road having given up completely. There was nothing to eat . . . absolute chaos . . . somehow he managed to get to Dunkirk . . . that's a port . . . and waited for two days and nights, hiding in the dunes when the German planes came over. Some of his friends were killed, some wounded . . . and if anyone got too panicky their sergeant pointed his gun at them and threatened to shoot if they didn't stay calm . . . And then, thank God, Daddy was rescued by a little ship because, as well as the Navy coming to help, hundreds of brave men and women sailed their own boats from England . . . just think of it! Hundreds of boats of all sizes from dinghies to the Navy's big ships went to rescue them, otherwise we might never have seen Daddy again . . .'

'Is that what we prayed about in church on Sunday?' asked Holly.

'Yes,' said Kitty. 'All over the country in every church everyone prayed that as many soldiers as possible could be rescued . . .'

'And they were . . .' said Holly.

'Yes,' said Kitty shakily. 'And they were . . . a miracle!'

And she began to cry.

Holly flung her arms round Kitty and hugged her.

'Don't cry, Mummy,' she said. 'You said we all had to be brave . . .' and then burst into tears herself, hardly knowing whether she was crying just for her father or for all those soldiers in the dunes, and those poor people with their children and their animals on those roads somewhere in France.

Meanwhile, the new term at Marlowes was under way and at prayers the boys sang as loudly as they could:

> *Fight the good fight with all thy might.*
> *Christ is thy strength and Christ thy might . . .*

And as Hugo moved his lips he prayed that he would not be noticed.

19
Holly's secret

Holly went to school too – all by herself, five miles each way on the bus, weighed down with a gas mask, a satchel and a music case.

Cars were no longer allowed for private purposes.

'What if there's an air raid while I'm on the bus?' she longed to ask Kitty. But did not dare. She somehow knew it would only make her mother cross.

She got to know the conductors and trusted they would look after her if there was an air raid. In fact, there never was and very soon she was going off happily each day. At Ash House School she could forget about missing her father and worrying about Hugo.

She loved marching into prayers, bending over her desk, her fingers coming to grips with pen and nibs and ink in china wells, filling up her exercise books with sums and spelling; she liked having to bow her head over shepherd's pie at lunchtime, the hot potato and meat smell wafting in the air as Miss Hobbs, the headmistress, said grace in a language Holly did not yet understand: *perJesumChristumDominumnostrum*.

She made friends with a girl called Jennifer who had also been evacuated and lived on a farm called Mop End near Marlowes. Soon they arranged to be on the same bus and Holly never tired of Jennifer's stories.

Holly longed to go and see Jennifer's white mice called Sissi and Piffi who were always having babies, and the cats that were always having kittens. But visiting after school and even in the holidays was impossible: it was too far to walk, buses were few and unreliable and there was an ever more real danger of air raids and of German planes dropping bombs in fields on their way home. Holly waited eagerly for the stories about the five "Mop End Kids".

'You'll never guess what happened yesterday,' Jennifer would say. 'The ceiling fell down when I was playing chopsticks!'

'Oh!' gasped Holly. 'Did you hurt yourself?'

'No, but it made a terrible mess,' said Jennifer. 'At first Mummy was really cross, but then she started laughing . . .!'

'We got into terrible trouble with Mr Hatt,' (Mr Hatt was the farmer). 'We were climbing on the beam in the barn, you see and Jonathan Jo – my little brother – fell off . . .'

'Oh! How awful!' cried Holly. 'Is . . . he . . . is he all right?'

'Oh, yes!' said Jennifer. 'He fell into a great pile of hay, but Mr Hatt told us all off. He says it's too dangerous for us to play up there, but, oh it's such fun! We went straight back the next day and when we heard Mr Hatt coming, we all hid behind the straw bales. "I know you're in there," he kept saying. "I know you're in there . . . Charles . . ."' (Charles was the eldest brother), '"Charles, you ought to know better!" But we just kept quiet till he gave up and went away and then we just rolled about laughing . . .'

Holly did not like it so much when Jennifer told her that Mr Hatt had wrung the neck of a baby wild rabbit with a broken leg.

'Oh,' she shuddered. 'Did you see him do it?'

'Oh yes,' said Jennifer. 'It was the kindest thing to do. It would have been much crueller to let it live in pain.'

Holly didn't think she had anything exciting to tell Jennifer about her life at Marlowes and was very surprised when Jennifer could not hear enough about going 'out of bounds', and Mr Pendleton throwing chalk at the boys; how Guy had been rescued by a 'Little Ship', and how Miles had gone and fetched Hugo from great danger in a faraway country. When she told her what Kitty had said about Jews, Jennifer said, 'Well, I can't see how they are any different from us . . . What about that girl, Rachel, in Upper II? She's come from London for safety and she's just like us, isn't she?'

'Yes,' Holly agreed.

At Greek dancing she made friends with Juliet, who

had long plaits and very red cheeks. They had both tried ballet and found they couldn't do it. Greek dancing was much nicer: Kitty had made Holly a silk tunic out of an old pink petticoat which she dyed green. You did not have to squeeze your feet into those narrow, unbending ballet shoes. You didn't have to wear any shoes at all. Juliet and Holly liked going barefoot and when the weather was hot and dry the class was held outside on the grass at a safe distance from other girls playing rounders. They got to play rounders too, of course, which Holly loved. She found she had a very good eye for batting and for catching the ball.

'I expect that's from all Imogen's French cricket,' laughed Kitty when Holly told her.

'Anyway that'll please Daddy – you can play cricket with him when the war is over!'

Holly was so happy she had made her mother smile at last that she ran up the stairs two at a time to get ready for bed.

One day there was an eclipse of the sun and Miss Eaton, the games teacher, gave them each a piece of smoky glass to look through. The sky went a very strange colour and the dull sunless light in the middle of a summer's day rather frightened the children.

Holly told her mother particles of her day, holding them up like patchwork pieces, a few at a time. She soon got used to her reply. 'Good, dear, good,' was all Kitty ever said. 'Just as long as you're happy and learning . . .'

'I've got a vocab book, now . . .' Holly told her.

'Vocab?' said Kitty, struggling with egg powder for scrambled eggs on toast covered with margarine.

'Yes, for French . . . I love French, Mummy . . .'

'Good, darling . . .'

'We make these long lists of words . . . I love saying them out loud . . . French is my best subject!'

'Good, darling,' her mother would say, as she darned her last pair of silk stockings, or counted out the last of the rock cakes.

Holly never told her mother about the bad things, like the time she got laughed at in gym. It was 'drill time' which meant standing in lines in your knickers and vest, doing exercises.

But Holly was in a dream, a dream about having a bicycle and going up that long straight lane and Jennifer being at the gate and Jennifer taking her to look at the kittens in the barn, and Jennifer helping her up on to that beam and daring her to walk across it and then jump into the hay . . .

'Holly!' came a sudden sharp voice. It was Miss Eaton.

'Stop daydreaming and pull your socks up!'

And Holly bent down and pulled up her socks, although they did not really need pulling up.

Then Miss Eaton laughed a nasty laugh and all the other girls turned and stared and laughed.

'Not your actual socks, dear!' said Miss Eaton sourly. 'I meant "put some vim into it"! Move, girl, move when I say so!'

Holly went red in the face and hot and cold and heard Miss Eaton's hiss of annoyance, as she tried to copy what the others were doing and found her arms had gone up when everyone else's had gone to the side.

She never told her mother how much she hated being seen in her knickers and vest. Because her piano lesson was straight after gym she had no time to change and had to run past the next class of older girls who were allowed to wear shirts and shorts. They always seemed to be laughing at her.

And then there was Miss Platt, the piano teacher, who had very greasy hair and smelt and got so cross with her because she always played B flat instead of B natural in Bach's *Minuet in G*.

And she never told her mother about taking Gillian's badge off her blazer in the cloakroom and breaking it.

Gillian was in the class above Holly. She was such a lively, talkative girl that Holly (whose father used to called her Little Miss Big Ears) could not help noticing her and hearing things she was saying to the crowd that was always gathered round her. She was always talking about France and the man who was now their leader, Marshal someone, who seemed to be on Hitler's side. Somehow Holly got the idea that the little gold badge Gillian always wore was an evil thing, something to do with Hitler being in France. The badge was cross-shaped, but not like the crosses she had seen in church. It had two bars across instead of one. The more she heard Gillian talking the more sure Holly became that she was on Hitler's side.

So one day at lunchtime when she had been allowed inside to go to the lavatory, she saw Gillian's blazer hanging on her peg and the little cross glinting on the lapel. Suddenly she found herself unpinning it and clutching it in her hand so hard it bent in two.

She was staring in horror at what she had done when she heard someone behind her.

'What are you doing with my badge?' It was Gillian.

'I . . . I . . . don't know,' trembled Holly, still staring at the broken cross. 'Give it to me,' Gillian commanded. Holly obeyed and Gillian put the cross in her tunic pocket.

'That was made by a friend of my parents. He makes them for the Free French to wear . . .'

'Oh,' muttered Holly, blushing scarlet. 'What's the Free French?'

'Don't you know anything about this war?' Gillian said crossly. 'The Free French are the ones who have escaped to England and are getting ready to go back and kick the Germans out of France.'

'You mean they're good?' asked Holly shakily.

'Of course they're good,' snapped Gillian. 'My parents' friend is French and he was asked to make the crosses by their leader, General de Gaulle, a very brave soldier. That's a cross, you fathead! Not a swastika! Oh dear I do believe you've muddled the cross up with Hitler's horrible swastika. What a baby! What an ignoramus!'

Holly began to cry.

'This is a very special cross which the French love,' Gillian explained. 'It is called the Cross of Lorraine because it comes from where Joan of Arc came from. Surely even you have heard of Joan of Arc?'

'Yes,' Holly nodded. 'I am so sorry,' she stammered. 'I am really really sorry . . . Perhaps we can unbend it?'

'No we jolly well can't,' said Gillian, at which Holly began to cry even more.

'Oh, do shut up!' sighed Gillian. 'It's not the end of the world. It's not real gold, you know! I can easily get another one . . .'

'Isn't it? Can you?' sobbed Holly.

'Yes,' said Gillian more gently. 'Well, I suppose at any rate it shows you hate Hitler as much as I do . . .' She started fishing around in her pockets and produced a scrap of paper and a stub of a pencil.

'Look, you'd better get to know what a swastika looks like, so you won't go breaking anybody else's crosses . . .'

And she quickly drew the thick, black, crooked cross, which Hitler had turned into a symbol of terror, suffering and death.

'Are you going to tell Miss Hobbs?' asked Holly anxiously.

'No,' said Gillian. 'Why should I? I caught you. You said you were sorry . . .'

'What about your friends?' trembled Holly.

Gillian was silent for a moment.

'Mm,' she said. 'I'll have to think about that . . .'

And that was all she would say.

But as the days went by and Gillian, with a new Cross of Lorraine on her blazer, now sometimes even said 'hello' to her in the corridors, Holly somehow got the feeling she had not said a word to anyone, and that she wasn't going to say a word to anyone.

Holly was grateful to Gillian and ashamed of herself. She buried what she had done deeply inside herself. She could not even have told Hugo about it. She had to bear it alone.

20

A narrow escape

'Darling Holly!' said Phoebe to Hereward one bedtime, dropping rings and hair-pins into one of Lady Marlowe's cut-glass bowls. 'When I told her I want to give her a bicycle she said Hugo must have one too!'

'Of course the boy must have a bike,' said Hereward. 'And I will teach him to ride it. The exercise will do him good . . . the boy, I suspect, *thinks* too much . . .'

'Of course he does!' exclaimed Phoebe, attacking her thick silvery hair with her silver-backed hairbrush. 'Poor child, he's got a lot to think about! I can't bear to think of his loneliness, his little homesick heart.'

Hereward plunged his hands into his dressing-gown pockets and stared out on to smooth lawns, studded with trees for sentinels, and in the distance the secret garden full of roses now in full bloom.

'He's not the only one here to suffer from this damned war,' he said at last. 'There are boys in this school whose fathers will go down with their ships . . . who will be mown down by machine-gunfire . . . who will fail to return from flying missions . . .'

'Don't!' gasped Phoebe, dropping her brush with a clatter.

'I'm sorry, my dear, but it will be so . . .'

Hereward put his arms round her and suddenly they were clinging to one another, picturing their own two sons as if they were children again.

'Ready, my dear?' murmured Hereward.

'Yes, dearest,' whispered Phoebe. And they knelt to pray as they did every night, like old children, one on each side of the bed.

'*Our Father*,' began Hereward, putting all into the hands of the Lord. '*Thy will be done* . . .'

And yet, and yet, insisted Phoebe silently . . . there *is* a difference . . . She felt it thinly, uncertainly. There *is* some terrible difference between the threat to the fathers of little English boys and the sense of menacing, unknown horror hovering over the world from which Miles and Guy had snatched Hugo Altman.

'*Deliver us from evil* . . .' prayed Hereward.

Phoebe saw words curling up out of smoke or black clouds. She saw hollow grey faceless figures with holes where mouths should be . . .

'*For thine is the kingdom, the power* . . .'

But she could not make out the words in the smoke, nor hear what the gaping holes were mouthing – a new language she would not anyway have understood, but which would eventually spell out F-i-n-a-l S-o-l-u-t-i-o-n.

'*And the glory for ever and ever, Amen . . .*'

They always knelt awhile in silence.

Then Phoebe got stiffly to her feet and said, 'So, we are agreed. Hugo must have a bicycle and I will see to it.'

She was as good as her word.

At the beginning of the summer holidays she bought bicycles for everyone and Dodo Church came to stay. She seemed far more out of place at Marlowes than she had on the ship coming from Africa. Phoebe tried not to stare at the bright green slacks and turban, and the ridiculously long red nails. It was if a parrot had landed screeching in Marlowes' green and pleasant land with its dull-coloured, familiar gatherings of pigeons, starlings and sparrows.

Whatever her private feelings about the visiting parrot, Phoebe and Hereward joined Dodo and Kitty in the earnest but often giggly matter of teaching Holly and Hugo to ride their bikes.

The evenings were wonderfully long thanks to the 'double summertime' intended to help the war effort by giving more daylight hours for factory workers and land girls.

At last the great moment came when Hugo and Holly were able to wobble safely down the long straight drive and confidently back again. Phoebe smiled upon them all – teachers and pupils – and produced a picnic for the children.

'Off you go now!' she cried, packing sandwiches and fizzy lemonade bottles into their bicycle baskets. 'Trial run! Have fun!'

As she recorded their departure with her Brownie box camera, Hereward raised his head from lighting his pipe and said to Hugo, 'Mm, and now you've mastered the bicycle I will initiate you into the secrets of bowling . . .'

When Hugo looked blank Phoebe said, crisply and too loudly, 'He means, dear, he will help you with your cricket.'

Hugo nodded palely.

'I rather paint a picture,' he said to Holly as they wobbled down the drive. 'I do not like cricket!' He rolled his rs dramatically and Holly giggled.

After she'd waved the children off, Phoebe turned to Kitty and Dodo.

'And now we have bicycles you girls will be able to get down to the village more often and make yourselves useful at the Officers' Club! All part of the war effort!'

One afternoon when Kitty and Dodo were down at the Officers' Club Phoebe took the children to a Red Cross fête.

On the bus Holly's greatest fear came true: the air-raid siren began to wail.

'Oh well, it's too late to turn back now,' said Phoebe. 'I'm not going back on our plan!'

She settled herself more solidly into her seat between Hugo and Holly.

'*I'm* the jam in the sandwich today!' she beamed.

Holly leaned against her grandmother's soft silk summer dress, sheltered beneath the brim of her large straw hat, and realised that she was no longer afraid.

'That's what you said in the car,' she said, fingering the tassels on Phoebe's parasol.

'Did I, dear?' said Phoebe vaguely.

'Yes, when we got off the ship from Africa, you remember? I was the jam then – that's what you said. I was sitting between you and Mummy . . . I was the jam in the sandwich . . .'

'Of course you were,' said Phoebe and drove her taffeta parasol straight as her own back into the corrugated runnel of the bus's floor.

Holly couldn't see Hugo's face; just his legs dangling down. Hugo wasn't frightened for himself in spite of the air-raid warning. But all the same the siren had chilled his heart. It reminded him of someone's mother wailing at that little airport far away and long ago.

'It'll be Slough again,' said the bus conductor, all knowing and offhand. 'They have to set the siren off in Woodham in case they scatter bombs on their way home, but it's Slough they're after with them factories an' all.'

'Poor, ugly Slough,' sighed Phoebe. 'And lovely old Windsor just next door. I hope the king and queen and the dear little princesses aren't at home . . .'

'Off to the fête, are you?' said the bus conductor. 'Should

123

be a good turn-out on such a lovely day – and for a good cause. Can't beat the Red Cross, that's what I say. Never been so glad to see their ambulance the day I was gassed in the last war . . .'

Suddenly the day seemed less warm, the bus conductor more ominous than the siren.

Holly's hand closed over her gas-mask box and Hugo stirred and mouthed questioningly to himself, 'Gassed . . . gassed?'

Phoebe grasped the ivory handle of her parasol with a regal twist of the wrist and leaned first to Holly and then to Hugo.

'Aren't we lucky this time!' she exclaimed. 'With these splendid gas masks for every man, woman and child in the land!'

Then and only then did she stare coldly at the bus conductor. 'It was a look fit to kill,' he told his wife that night. 'She went all hoity-toity, sitting there with her back stiff as a plank, with her fancy umbrella! Quite put me in mind of old Queen Mary!'

And when the all clear went he offered it to Phoebe like a pipe of peace.

'There goes the all clear,' he said, as if only he could hear its reassuring descent down a major key.

But Phoebe ignored him.

'You can ring the bell, Holly, when I tell you.'

People were streaming into the garden of the house

where the fête was being held, completely unconcerned by the nearby air raid. The Home Guard stood by, unable to see an excuse to marshal their troops.

The children lingered at the stalls of home-made humbugs and misshapen barley sugar sticks.

'Later,' Phoebe said. 'Later, I promise. We want to be sure of good seats for the concert.'

She steered them into the crowd heading for the deck chairs set up round a makeshift bandstand, where old soldiers were tinkering with trumpets and tuning up drums.

'Lovely!' cried Phoebe. She shooed Holly and Hugo ahead of her. 'A few old tunes is what we need to buck us up a bit!'

'Will there be tea?' asked Holly. 'You said there'd be tea.'

'Tea's indoors – to keep the wasps away from the jam. We'll save tea till last. Goodness! What a lot of tooting and blasting and spitting!'

She settled them, one on each side of her, in the second row of chairs, wishing she felt able to ease off her rarely worn summer shoes.

'And we mustn't forget to buy some bottled fruit for Mummy,' said Phoebe. 'After all, we are here to raise money . . .'

What funny things grown-ups say, Holly thought, knowing now not to expect pound notes to start sprouting from the flower-beds. It was like 'Guy has been posted abroad' – her father posted to India by the Army like a letter. It was like 'pull your socks up' in gym.

'Ahh!' Phoebe breathed. 'Here comes the conductor . . .'

Hugo too was tussling with the English language. 'Conductor?' The man on the bus with the machine which went click and turned out pink tickets – he was 'conductor'. Now this man standing in front of the musicians, holding up a stick which had made a small but exciting silence fall – was he too 'conductor'?

But before the band could say 'Goodbye to the girls they'd left behind them', or 'pack up their troubles in their old kit bag and smile, smile, smile', the drone of a bluebottle filled the hot sky. A mutant, metallic bluebottle with black crosses on the tips of its wings.

It flew low over the garden, rat-tatting like an overwound clockwork woodpecker devised by an insane toymaker.

'Take cover!' sharp voices commanded. 'Down! Everybody down! Lie down!'

Up went Phoebe's parasol as she plummeted beneath the deck chairs, pulling Holly under one arm, Hugo under the other until they were pressed up against her like chicks under a mother hen.

What a big bum she's got, thought Holly, feeling a giggle begin as she was being dragged down. The giggle died as she realised Phoebe's parasol would not protect them from bullets. She began to shiver and shake and her teeth to chatter so violently and loudly she felt the gun noise was in her mouth.

I must not get killed, thought Hugo. *Please God don't let me get killed. I want to see Mama and Papa again.* He cowered closer to Phoebe and for the rest of his life smelt fear in new-mown grass.

The rat-tat stopped. The drone faded. Silence lay over the lawn. Pressed against the earth he heard heavy feet running, stumbling, clumping about. He dared not look up.

But Holly turned her head and opened her eyes. The soldiers were moving from body to body, touching shoulders, urging people to their feet.

'Nobody hurt!' came the call from each part of the garden.

'It's a miracle, a bloody miracle!'

Tense, gritty voices snapped backward and forwards.

Holly saw a bumble-bee drowse into a hollyhock.

'Right!' barked a man used to giving orders. 'Everybody into the house! And run! Run like hell!'

'Bloody bastards!' yelled another soldier. 'But they missed, didn't they? Missed us all, bloody Gerry bastards, firing on innocent women and children!'

'Innocent.' Hugo did not try to say it. The word trembled into him. Innocent. *Unschuldig.* Somehow he knew that was him and Holly and Mrs Nash and all these people on the green lawn and all those people at that airport long ago. Innocent.

The Home Guard were the last to come into the dark, stuffy house.

Through the clamour of anger and questions and small

127

ripples of hysteria and whimpering, the tea urn gurgled.

'That's it,' said one of the men. 'Is someone brewing us all a nice cuppa?'

And as the cups clattered and women let their teeth chatter in breathless, broken sentences, the plane came back.

'Godstrewth!' cursed a soldier.

'On the floor everyone!' came the order. 'And keep away from the windows!'

But this time the voice was not obeyed.

Everyone simply stood and stared out of the diamond-paned windows.

Someone dropped a teaspoon on to the parquet floor.

The plane wheeled away.

And they waited.

And waited.

Five minutes. Ten minutes. A petrifying quarter of an hour.

'He'll not be back now,' promised a soldier.

Others went outside, gazed at the sky a good while, then began to pick up and count the bullets that peppered the lawn.

Phoebe became bossy, ordering other women to pass round tea.

'Of course you'll have scones and jam. I promised,' she said to Holly and Hugo. 'Or at least one rock cake,' she said, thrusting food upon them which now tasted like sugared ashes on their trembling tongues. 'And then we'll go straight home.'

Suddenly her legs seemed to have turned to jelly, but somehow she marched them to the gates, praying with all her heart that they would not have long to wait for a bus.

'You look after us always, Mrs Nash,' said Hugo tremulously.

'Of course I do,' said Phoebe. 'Of course I do! That's what I'm for!' She felt for her handkerchief, and wiped her eyes.

'We're all right, Grandmamma!' said Holly, slipping her hand into Phoebe's clammy palm. 'Don't cry, don't cry,' she said.

On the bus Phoebe dozed over her parasol.

'It was a real ad-adventure!' Hugo whispered to Holly behind Phoebe's bowed back.

'Yes,' Holly agreed. 'I can't wait to tell Jennifer!'

21
'Where are the mothers?'

Halfway up the drive Phoebe and the children could hear laughter coming from the garden of the butler's house.

A combat knife was still juddering in the trunk of the old apple tree as Holly rushed ahead of the others.

'We were machine-gunned!' Holly announced to Kitty and Dodo and the circle of Army officers they must have brought back from the club. 'And Grandmamma saved our lives!' Phoebe had heard the laughter, seen Kitty and Dodo and the crowd of young men, sprawled on the lawn, their highly-polished leather belts gleaming in the sun. She was inclined to sweep on, but Kitty had broken away from the crowd.

'Wh-what?' Kitty croaked, her face very pale.

The young men had leapt to their feet, the smiles instantly wiped from their faces and suddenly seemed to be standing to attention. Dodo lit a cigarette and avoided everybody's eyes.

'We heard the siren, of course,' stammered Kitty, 'but I didn't worry . . . I thought it must be Slough.'

'It was Slough,' said Phoebe curtly.

'A wandering bandit?' asked one of the officers. 'Isn't that what the RAF call those German rotters scattering ammunition any old where after a raid?'

'Yes, a wandering bandit – couldn't have put it better myself,' snapped Phoebe, 'but – as you see – all's well that ends well. Finish your fun. I will keep the children with me till their suppertime.'

In the house Phoebe took off her hat in front of a mirror which reflected the little pale faces behind her.

'Now, off you go and wash your hands!' she said briskly. 'And Hugo – don't forget to lift the seat. A gentleman always lifts the seat. I'm just going upstairs for a minute. Then we'll go to the rose garden. That will soothe us all . . .'

'Soothe,' murmured Hugo, as he dried his hands carefully on a thin towel. 'Soothe . . .'

Holly rushed past him into the downstairs cloakroom to empty her bursting fear-filled bladder.

Phoebe slipped into Lady Marlowe's sitting-room, poured herself a nip of brandy and took down a copy of *The Wind in the Willows*.

Then she marched the children to the rose garden, and settled herself on the bench in front of the little pavilion. Holly and Hugo flopped down at her feet on the warm bricks like tired puppies and Phoebe began to read.

Drowsily Holly and Hugo heard about water and trees, the quiet boat rocking, some loving creature smiling on Rat and Mole, sweet piping music, finding what was lost, forgetting what was too strong to bear, being tired, being taken care of . . .

Then Hugo opened his eyes and knelt up beside her and said, 'But, Mrs Nash, where are the mothers?'

'What, dear?' asked Phoebe, startled.

'The mothers. Where are the mothers?'

'I never thought of that before!' said Phoebe brightly. 'It is true – there are no mothers in this story . . .'

'Why don't I get any letter any more from my mother?' Hugo broke in.

'Well, dear . . .' Phoebe stumbled, then firmed her voice, tried to sound stern. 'Just think about that for a minute. You're not a baby. You know the Germans are everywhere, fighting and making trouble – everywhere – not just in your country. How could the poor postman collect letters? How could he send them to us now? You are not the only pebble on the beach . . . There must be lots of other children who would like letters too . . . and anyway, you mustn't give up hope . . .'

But Hugo wasn't listening. His eyes were full of tears. He was back in the dark Prague apartment with its heavy, solid furniture and the smell of fresh coffee, of caraway, of dumplings and rich meat stew.

'In the night,' he quavered, 'I think of my mother very much . . .'

Phoebe dropped the book and flung her arms round the boy.

'Oh, Hugo . . .' And she rocked him close against her, staring past him blindly.

Holly suddenly felt wildly jealous of Hugo being cuddled and comforted by her grandmother. *He's not the only one*, she thought. *My mother is only on the other side of this wall, but she might just as well be in another country sometimes. I suppose she loves me . . . I suppose she does . . .*

But now Phoebe stood up and held out a hand to Holly.

'Darling . . .' she murmured as if she knew what Holly was thinking. *Like when she got the bikes*, thought Holly.

'Let's look at the roses!' she said.

Holly and Hugo trailed after Phoebe past the beds thick with roses and the scent of roses, some white, some pink, some yellow, some almost as black as dried blood.

Phoebe leaned over to smell a large bloom.

'*Peace*!' she breathed. '*Peace*!' Isn't that a lovely name?'

Half-heartedly the children bent to smell, but she had already moved on.

'But this is what I call a real rose, an old rose . . . see how close the rose grows to the huge cruel thorns? Of course, it won't last long . . . no, it will go over quite soon, but how beautiful while it lasts!' Her voice shook with joy, sorrow, defiance. 'Smell it, children! The fragrance of an old rose will stay with you for ever, and whenever, wherever you smell it you will find yourselves straight back here . . .'

22

Panic

The grown-ups had been thoroughly rattled by what had happened at the fête. Phoebe even stayed in bed the next morning, announcing that she needed a little rest.

'Why don't you get the butterfly nets out?' she suggested to Hereward. 'I doubt Hugo ever caught a Purple Emperor in the heart of Prague . . .'

Over in the butler's house Kitty was saying to Holly, 'You're a big girl now, big enough to help a bit. I want you to take this duster every morning after breakfast and go round all the rooms – carefully, mind!'

'You can start in my room,' yawned Dodo. 'I always seem to get my face powder over everything . . .'

And the two women went off on their bikes, Dodo with a mysterious smile.

'We won't be long, ducky! If you're a good girl there'll be a surprise for you later!'

Kitty added, 'And when you've finished dusting, don't

disturb Grandmamma today. Go and join Granddad and Hugo – I've just seen them heading for the garden.'

Up in Dodo's room Holly powdered her nose and sneezed. She tried Dodo's hair curlers – funny things rather like brown pipe-cleaners. She flicked the duster about a bit, as she had seen her mother do, moving dust from here to there, and longed to stick her little finger in the rouge pot and rub a little on her cheeks.

Then she saw the ring: five milky stones swirling with green and red like petrol in a puddle.

She tried it on. It slipped round loosely, so she stuck it on her thumb and held her hand out at a distance to admire it, as she had seen Kitty do when she was drying her varnished nails.

Then Hereward called to her from the garden.

Holly jumped, and ran to the window waving her duster.

Hugo was there too, hanging back behind Hereward's solid form.

'Good girl!' called Hereward. 'Been helping your mother? How about coming down and helping me teach Hugo how to catch butterflies?'

Dropping her duster, Holly dashed eagerly downstairs and watched with Hugo as her grandfather stalked a flock of Cabbage Whites hovering over the flowering peas and beans. He singled one out, raised his net and ensnared the fluttering creature.

'Got you!' he shouted. 'See?' he said, turning to the

children. 'Easy, eh? And jolly good fun! When I was a boy I had the finest butterfly collection in the West Country . . . moths, too.'

'What will you now do with the butterfly?' asked Hugo carefully.

'Why, kill it, of course!' said Hereward.

'Kill?' faltered Hugo.

'Yes,' said Holly. 'You put it in that jar . . . there's ether in it . . .'

'The ether finishes it off,' Hereward put in. 'Quick and painless.'

'Ether?' repeated Hugo. 'Finishes it off?'

'Yes . . . a sort of gas,' said Hereward patiently.

'Gas,' echoed Hugo. 'Gas . . .'

He just stood there staring.

Holly moved to stand beside him.

The children stared at Hereward, at the Cabbage White trapped in the net, at the jar, empty, waiting, sinister.

'When it is dead,' said Hugo, 'what then do you do with the butterfly?'

'Well,' said Hereward, 'taking care not to touch the wings, so as not to spoil their bloom, you pin it neatly through the middle of its body on to a tray and keep it covered under glass, so it does not fall to pieces . . .'

Hugo stared at the butterfly.

'No!' he gasped. 'No! Please Mr Nash, do not kill it! It wants to go – up there . . .' His hands fluttered out and up like wings. 'It wants to live ... Up there – away – somewhere good and free!'

He began to cry.

'Let it go, Mr Nash! Please! Please, let it go!'

'All right, old chap, all right!' said Hereward, hastily releasing the butterfly. 'No need to get so upset. But Cabbage Whites are pests, you know! They eat our vegetables! Don't the boys and girls in Czechoslovakia catch butterflies?'

'I don't know!' sobbed Hugo. 'But I will not.'

He brushed past Holly and Hereward and ran into the house.

'Oh dear,' said Hereward in dismay. 'Oh dear. Holly, perhaps you'd better go to him.'

When he was alone he mopped his head with his handkerchief. 'Poor boy,' he mused. 'He'll have to toughen up, or he'll find the world a cruel place . . .'

Holly went after Hugo and knelt by the sofa where he was lying, his head buried in the cushions.

'Don't cry,' she begged him. 'Don't cry!'

She put out a hand to touch his.

'Oh!' she gasped, terror running up her spine. 'The ring! It's gone! Hugo!'

She shook him. 'I've lost Auntie Dodo's ring! Hugo, help me!'

Hugo emerged slowly from the cushions.

'Ring?'

'Yes! I put it on my thumb when I was dusting and now it's gone! Oh, help me to find it before she comes back!'

Hugo sat up, rubbing his swollen eyes.

'You waved from the window,' he said.

'Yes, I know,' said Holly impatiently. 'I know I did. I waved the duster to you and Granddad.'

'Come!' said Hugo, jumping up from the sofa, glad to be in charge, to be needed. He made for the front door out into the garden.

'Let us look in the flowers, under the window, where you waved.'

He was already on his knees, gently parting leaves.

'You are clever!' said Holly, squatting down beside him.

'What colour is the ring?' asked Hugo.

'Milky,' said Holly, 'with green and pink in it.'

'This?' said Hugo, triumphantly holding up Dodo's opal ring.

'Yes!' breathed Holly with relief. 'You are clever! Thank you! What would I have done without you?'

Hugo looked pleased.

'Quick!' he hissed, passing the ring to Holly. 'Put it back . . . be sure it is in the same place . . . I will watch from down here.'

'Whistle if they come,' said Holly.

'What?' said Hugo.

'Oh, you know,' said Holly, pursing up her lips, 'like this . . . whistle!'

When Kitty and Dodo returned, they found Hugo pushing Holly on the old swing which hung rather drunkenly from a branch of the old apple tree.

'Surprise! Surprise!' called Dodo sounding friendly and excited.

'Come along, you two!' Kitty sang out. 'Come and see what we've got for you!'

The surprise was rabbits – a pair of babies, quivering and twitching in fresh straw in an old hutch the children had never really noticed among the potting sheds along the cinder path.

'One each!' said Kitty. 'Something for you to look after.'

'To keep you out of mischief,' added Dodo with a wink.

Holly and Hugo were speechless with happiness.

Dodo opened the hutch and laid a rabbit into each pair of nervously outstretched hands.

'They scratch!' whispered Holly.

'It's their little claws in those furry paws,' said Dodo, and she showed them how to stroke the long, quivering, silky ears with one hand cupped gently under the soft, trembling bodies.

'It'll be up to you to keep them fed and change their water and their bedding,' said Kitty.

'What shall we call them?' said Holly, turning to Hugo.

'How about Bubble and Squeak?' suggested Dodo. 'They're such a mixture of white and dark, reminds me of that fry-up your mother makes of potatoes and greens!'

'Yes, yes!' Holly and Hugo chorused. Anything Dodo suggested was all right. Anything!

They bowed their happy, relieved heads over the rabbits and stroked them tenderly.

'Bubble,' murmured Hugo.

'Squeak,' whispered Holly.

23

War games

'Dogfight!' yelled Hugo's friend, Browning.

They had stayed friends since the far-off time in Swanstown when they had collected conkers together. And now their friendship was deeper than ever. Browning's father had gone down with his ship, the aircraft carrier, *Courageous*, in the Bristol Channel. They never talked to each other about their sorrows, but liked doing things together. Browning was helping Hugo to start a stamp collection; Hugo was teaching him to draw tanks and aeroplanes.

Hugo looked round. No dogs. What dogs? There were no dogs at Marlowes.

'Dogfight? Where?' he asked.

'Oh Lor', Altman, not real dogs, you ass!' said Browning. 'Up there! Planes! One German, one English. Look! Up there! Wow! I say, I think he's got him!'

Hugo stared up into the bright blue autumn sky. Yes, he saw them now – two planes right up close to each other, smoke streaming from one as it began to plummet down the sky . . . aeroplanes, not dogs, so why say dogs? He would never understand this language, but as he watched the two planes circling one another they did remind him of dogs sizing each other up before a fight.

'Wow!' yelled Browning. 'Yes, he has got him!' But impossible to tell who had got who. The silvery little planes were much too far away for the reality of a fight between two men to the death to reach the small boys in grey watching on the Marlowes lawn. Nor could they know they were watching a fragment of The Battle of Britain, Spitfires and Hurricanes against the huge German Air Force.

The phoney war was definitely over.

The Blitz had begun. Night and day for many months the Germans dropped their bombs on London, not caring where they fell.

Marlowes was only thirty miles away and suddenly did not seem very safe.

Hereward offered himself as an air-raid warden, which meant being ready to take care of everyone else if there was an air raid. Constance sent Imogen down to stay while her school hastily set about evacuating itself to Wales, and Robert Pendleton somehow got hold of a noisy old film projector.

At Marlowes, after supper, sometimes even on school nights, everyone gathered in the ballroom to watch Mickey

Mouse, Goofy, or Felix the Cat. Hereward wanted what he called 'a camouflage against fear'.

Jerking uncertainly on a screen, improvised in a white space, where some great painting had hung till packed away for safety, the cartoons were something to hide behind.

For behind that screen on the ballroom wall, behind the heavy velvet curtains, behind the sticky paper criss-crossed over the windows, London was flickering with imprecise, uncontrollable flames. People were sheltering in the Underground every night, without heat or lavatories, trying to sleep on escalators and stone-cold platforms, being bombed out of their homes, being killed. Night after night, orderly searchlights tried to trap the bombers in their great beams so that the anti-aircraft guns in the royal parks could perhaps shoot them down.

At Marlowes the camouflage against fear sometimes wore thin: the boys and girls watching the rather cruel capers of Felix the Cat would grow fidgety and then there was baiting and bullying.

One evening when Imogen started pulling Holly's plaits and whispering, 'Holly, Holly looks like a silly Dutch dolly,' a hand shot out and closed over her wrist.

'Don't do this!' said Hugo.

Imogen stuck out her tongue.

Holly turned round and tried to find Hugo's eyes in the flickering light, but dared not look too long. She thought of the rose garden and wished they were both there now, in

143

bright, warm daytime, leaning against Phoebe, hearing the blackbirds sing.

'Gosh, you really are gone on each other, aren't you?' hissed Imogen.

From her armchair at the side of the room Phoebe fought sleep and laid a reproving finger to her lips.

After the films Holly and Imogen trailed behind the boys down the wide corridor. Hugo lagged behind a little, but he did not look back.

Imogen was chattering, but Holly saw an older boy slip behind the long curtains, saw stout black shoes peeping beneath the hem, saw the bigger boy fling out, fall on Hugo and pin him to the ground. She kicked the bully in the shins, she scratched the bully face.

'Let go!' she screamed. 'Let go!'

'Little spitfire!' jeered the bully, backing off, crossing his fingers mockingly. '*Pax*! *Pax*! Okay! Get up, brat!' he said to Hugo. 'If you weren't a girl,' he sneered at Holly, 'first chance I'd get I'd grind you into the gravel out there.' He jerked his head towards the paths that lay beyond the blacked-out windows.

Hugo had vanished into the grey uniform mass of boys his own size.

Imogen was jealous. She was the tomboy, the climber of trees; she went to school with boys; was used to them; it was her parents who fought for the weak, the helpless.

'Gosh!' she said, sidling up to Holly. 'You're strong for

such a skinny little thing. Are you gone on Hugo?'

'What?' said Holly.

'You know, have you got a crush on him?' Imogen poked Holly in the ribs and sniggered. 'Are you going to marry him one day?'

'Shut up,' said Holly.

But Imogen didn't shut up.

'Holly *aime* Hugo!' she chanted, dancing alongside her cousin to the laughter of the older boys coming up behind them. '*Et* Hugo *aime* Holly.'

She made disgusting kissing noises with her lips until Phoebe swooped down on the two girls, shooing them before her like a mother hen. 'Girls! Girls! This is a school after all. If you can't behave better than that no more Felix the Cat for you!'

24
Don't let him die

And now began a long dark time. The war grew grimmer and grimmer as Hitler spread his dark force over more and more of the world. He marched into Russia and there in the deep snow and ice, soldiers and ordinary people fought to survive, ready to eat anything, dogs, cats, rats, even their own leather belts and boots, but more often dying from cold and starvation. The Japanese decided to copy Hitler. First they bombed the neutral American Navy out of the water at Pearl Harbor. Then they began to invade Burma, Malaya and the islands of the Pacific, terrorising everyone in their path. They tormented the soldiers of the Allied forces who rose up to fight them in the never-ending, snake-filled, steaming jungle. If they were captured they were forced, although ill and starving, to build railways and bridges in the merciless heat. Miles's ship was still escorting convoys across the Atlantic. From India Guy wrote that things had livened up now that Japan was in the war.

And at Marlowes Hugo fell seriously ill.

Very early on a bitterly cold morning, before the other boys were up, Hugo was carried over to the butler's house by Robert Pendleton.

'It's pneumonia,' whispered Robert. 'The doctor's just left.'

'Come through quickly,' said Kitty tersely. 'It's freezing out here. It's the room at the top of the stairs . . .'

There was a small shivery moan from somewhere above them.

Robert's eyes followed Kitty's up the stairwell where Holly stood staring down, clutching the banister knob. She had heard the doorbell.

'What are you doing out of bed?' snapped Kitty up the stairwell. 'Go back to your room at once. Do you want to catch your death of cold? Hugo is very ill. I'm going to have my work cut out nursing him. You are not to go into his room, do you hear?'

Robert's arms tightened briefly round the sick boy. For a moment he had the wild idea of nursing Hugo himself in his quiet room. How could he surrender him into this chill house? He was being fanciful of course, and set foot firmly on the first step of the stairs. Kitty Nash, after all, was a capable woman and a mother.

'I lit the fire earlier,' Kitty resumed her whispering. 'Phoebe slipped over to warn me he was worse. The room's nice and warm now, though God knows how we'll keep it so with our meagre coal rations.'

But God did know and through the vicar's mild but persuasive voice at Morning Service wrought a small miracle.

'I know I can ask you for another sacrifice in our war against the forces of evil,' he appealed to the villagers from the pulpit. 'There's a little lad up at the school come down with pneumonia . . . And you all know what that means: warmth, careful nursing, and prayer that one day a medicine will be found to combat this killer. What's more the lad is a bit of a special case . . . a refugee from Hitler, no less – a waif in a strange land. Spare a thought for his parents, wherever they may be. A child's a child, a mother's a mother the whole world over. So, how about some coal to keep that sickroom warm – just till he turns the corner which with God's help he will, not to say with the first-rate nursing Mrs Guy Nash is putting in night and day. So I can leave it to you, I know . . . All contributions gratefully received . . . Thank you and pray God he pulls through. We will now sing *Onward Christian Soldiers*, Hymn number 48 in the green book.'

He looked encouragingly at his congregation, and led them loudly in the singing.

For several days Holly obeyed Kitty.

Always, as she reached the icy landing, she could smell the warm sickliness seeping under the door like cloying gas – vomit, Dettol and medicine, and stuffiness from windows tightly closed.

Sometimes she heard Hugo coughing and retching.

Then she would run to her room and cover her ears, flinging herself to her knees by the bed.

'Please, God,' she would sob. 'Please, God, don't let him die.'

Her prayer was not cosy. Not like the mechanical bedtime repetition of the Lord's Prayer after the quick bath in the miserable ration of five inches of tepid water in a bathroom so cold that face cloths could freeze.

Suddenly Holly knew: there was no kind God looking like Granddad Nash up there in the sky. There was just silence and perhaps no God at all. Hugo would get better or he would die. Nothing to do with God. It seemed silly to be asking, but she still went on asking: 'Don't let him die . . . Don't let him die . . .'

Holly could see that her mother was doing her best to get Hugo better even if she didn't love him. She found her in the kitchen making lemon barley water. Sometimes through the open sickroom door she saw her bathing Hugo's forehead, or lifting him higher on to the pillows, or stoking the fire. She never heard her comforting him, but her grandmother came in every day and sometimes she heard her singing to him softly.

The crisis came with the first crocuses.

Holly woke up one morning under her thin blankets to find Phoebe in the doorway, holding a steaming pink pudding bowl.

'He's turned the corner!' she whispered. 'I'm taking him bread and milk – your granddad's favourite. Perhaps later today your mother will let you put your head round the door – just for a minute.'

Holly felt warm for the first time for many days.

After lunch Kitty made herself a hot-water bottle and slid into well-earned sleep under her slippery satin eiderdown.

Holly crept down the passage and into Hugo's room.

He lay propped on several pillows. He was very pale and shrunken, his eyes closed, a narrow bony wrist jutting inches out of the pyjama cuff.

The fire was low. Holly picked up one lump of coal and dropped it with a crash on to the embers.

Hugo opened his eyes and smiled at her.

'I will be better now,' he said weakly, and began to cough.

'Holly! For God's sake! Leave the boy alone!'

Kitty was standing in the door.

'What did I tell you? Out you go, my girl! Haven't I had enough trouble? Do you want your precious Hugo to have a relapse? And leave that fire alone! Just look at your fingers! Go and wash your hands at once! Come along! Leave the boy in peace and let me get some rest.'

She seized Holly by the elbow and propelled her out of the room, pulling the door shut roughly.

'I don't want to see you till teatime. Go and play with your doll or something.'

'Her leg's broken,' quavered Holly.

'Too bad,' said Kitty.

But some days later, when it was clear that Hugo was much better, Kitty relented.

Holly was allowed to be there when Robert Pendleton came to visit Hugo.

He brought with him a knife and some small bits of wood.

He sat on a chair by the bed and showed Hugo how to whittle little figures out of the wood.

'Well!' said Kitty admiringly. 'If you are a toymaker, perhaps you are also a toymender! Holly's doll has a broken leg.'

She prodded Holly.

'Well, go on, darling! Run and fetch your invalid.'

She was kneeling now by the fire, triumphant and relaxed.

'See,' she said to Robert, 'he's much, much better and he's had a letter from home!'

'Good, good!' said Robert Pendleton, smiling at Hugo, who was scraping rather fiercely at a piece of wood.

Kitty turned from poking the fire.

'I think we can be a little reckless now, don't you? With the last of the coal, I mean. Hugo will soon be running about again. Let's make hot, buttered toast and go out in a blaze! Hugo! It's time you got out of bed for a bit to stretch those legs. That's it, Holly! Give the toymender your doll and then run down and fetch the toasting fork. Yes! You heard! We're going to have some fun!'

'And cocoa?' said Robert Pendleton mock-wistfully.

'And cocoa!' laughed Kitty, scrambling to her feet.

'Do you want any help?'

'No, I've got Holly. Just keep an eye on Hugo while you fix that doll's leg. And don't let the fire go out!'

Deftly Robert hooked the doll's leg back into place and looked up.

Hugo was sitting on the edge of the bed staring at him.

Never had he seen such sorrow in a child's eyes.

He held out a flimsy bit of paper. 'I had this . . .'

He handed it to Robert who saw it was a form rather like a telegram and had come from the International Red Cross. Addressed to the boy c/o Mrs Nasch, Hugo's parents' printed message was chilling for what it did not say: *Before our journey, many kisses. Be brave. Have our numbers. Write to Anne, your aunt . . .*

'Well,' said Robert rather too brightly, 'you must be jolly glad to hear from them. It's been a long time, hasn't it?'

'Yes,' said Hugo. 'But . . . why is it not just an ordinary letter?'

'Well, I don't know the answer to that,' said Robert, 'but I do know the Red Cross is always there to be helpful in times of war, perhaps the Post Office isn't working properly?'

But Hugo just stared at him baldly.

'I do not know what it means – a journey, numbers . . .'

'I don't know what it means, either,' Robert admitted.

'I want to go home,' Hugo said quietly. 'I want my mother.'

'I know, Altman,' said Robert gently. 'I know . . .'

'I want to give her this, now!'

Hugo held out his first uncertain, clumsy carving. Great tears were falling on to his thin hands, staining his pyjama legs.

'Yes, Altman, I know,' said Robert, clearing his throat and trying to sound brisk and matter-of-fact. 'All in good time. Come on, boy! You heard what Mrs Nash said. Time to stretch your legs, so let's see you on your feet. You want to be fighting fit for your mother, don't you?'

'Yes, sir,' said Hugo, stepping feebly on to the floor.

'You wouldn't want her to see you looking like a skeleton would you? A bag of skin and bones, would you?'

'No, sir.'

'You'd like to take her some first-class carvings, wouldn't you?'

'Yes, sir.'

'Right then! Three turns round the room and you can have my share of the buttered toast!'

'Thank you . . . and, sir? Will you show me how to make birds? I would like to make many birds for my mother.'

'Right you are, Altman! But first you've got to buck up, eh? Get well enough to go back to school, so we can get on with the carving.'

'Yes, sir,' said Hugo.

Suddenly he felt he must get better as quickly as possible. If he started to make the birds everything would be all right. His mother would come . . . he would give them to her . . . she would love them . . . his father would put them on a special shelf . . .

When Robert left him Hugo lay back on the pillows and fell into a deep, deep sleep.

25

Holly overhears

When at long last the summer holidays came round again, Kitty took Holly and Hugo on a flying visit to Dodo Church.

They had to change trains in London where silvery barrage balloons drifted in thick clusters overhead.

'They look like fat fish,' said Holly. 'And the sky is like a new bright blue sea . . .'

'What are they for?' asked Hugo.

'To stop the German planes,' said Kitty.

'They're as big as whales!' said Holly.

'With elephant ears!' suggested Hugo.

They piled into a train already crowded with soldiers cramming the compartments and corridors. Their cigarette smoke, thick uniforms and noisy banter clogged the hot August air.

When one of the soldiers offered his seat to Kitty, all the others clapped, but the children had to stand all the way.

They were only too happy when it was time to get off the

train to find Dodo waiting for them with a pony and trap. 'Someone lent it to me,' she explained. 'Used to have one of these when I was a kid!'

'So did I!' said Kitty happily.

'You never told me that before!' said Holly.

'There are a lot of things I haven't told you yet!' said Kitty.

Dodo set the pony off at a good trot and soon they were hanging on for dear life, but enjoying every minute of it.

Dodo lived in a cottage. Oriental and African nick-nacks jostled among china shepherdesses and spaniels on dressers and in fussy cabinets.

'How are the bunnies?' she asked, as she poured them all a cool drink of lemonade.

Holly looked at Hugo. Hugo looked at Holly.

'They're very well, thank you,' said Holly, restraining herself from telling the whole story in case Hugo did not want her to show him up.

But Hugo was feeling happy. He liked Dodo and even he could see it was a funny story – now.

'They had babies!' said Hugo. 'Only I did not at first understand that they were babies. I thought that Bubble and Squeak had broken into lots of little pieces.'

'What?' laughed Dodo.

'He went to feed them,' said Holly, 'and then he came

156

running back and he was crying and saying, "Come quickly! Come quickly!" '

'So we all rushed to the hutch,' put in Kitty, 'and there's Hugo sobbing, "They're broken! They're broken!" Of course I took one look and saw what had happened . . . five dear little Bubbles and Squeaks!'

'My godfathers!' exclaimed Dodo. 'You poor old thing, Hugo! That must have given you quite a fright!'

Hugo nodded.

'Silly boy!' said Kitty, but quite kindly.

'Well,' said Holly sticking up for her friend, 'I bet I would have thought the same – neither of us had ever seen baby animals before and how little they are and all . . . all . . .'

'Wrrriggly,' Hugo brought out triumphantly, rolling his r's dramatically.

'What on earth did you do with them all?' asked Dodo.

'We gave them away,' said Hugo sadly.

'To some of my friends at school,' sighed Holly.

'Oh well,' laughed Dodo. 'There'll be a next time . . .'

'Will there?' said Hugo.

'Don't!' groaned Kitty.

And the women smiled at one another, while Holly tried to explain to Hugo that Bubble and Squeak might break into little pieces again.

'Now,' said Dodo, 'I've made you kids a little supper, and then, my ducks, straight to bed! But you'll have to share a bedroom, I'm afraid.'

She looked at Kitty rather anxiously.

'Oh well,' said Kitty. 'It is only for one night.'

Dodo took the children upstairs to a bedroom under the sloping cottage roof. There was a door at the bottom of the stairs which she left open.

'Stifling, isn't it?' she said, flinging the little windows wide open. 'You'll only need sheets. This double summertime! Sun won't be down for hours, but try to go to sleep. Count sheep or something and tomorrow we'll go to the fair. Might take you on the Ghost Train! Nighty-night!'

Holly and Hugo lay obediently beneath the sheets in the stuffy little room overlooking Dodo's garden. They heard the two women settling themselves out there, the clink of glasses and plates. Holly crept to the window and, keeping her head down, peeped out. They were sitting having supper at a little table. They had kicked off their shoes. A soda siphon stood in the grass.

Hugo fell asleep quickly, but Holly lay there, tossing and turning. She lay there listening to the bubbly laughter floating up from the garden, the tinkle of glass, the clatter of knives and forks.

And then she heard her mother say, 'I can't help it, I just don't love her the way I know I should . . . I think of the little boy every day . . . If I had been there . . . I can't believe he would have died . . . I would have noticed long before anyone that he was ill . . . I would have known . . .'

'But, darling, it sounds as if nothing, no one could have saved him. It's hardly Holly's fault, poor kid . . .'

'I know,' said Kitty, 'I know it's not her fault, but somehow knowing doesn't make any difference to how I feel . . . angry . . . angry with everyone.'

'Well, it's in the past now. A terrible tragedy. Nobody's fault . . . In the past now . . . Holly's a sweet child . . . Drink up, darling.' Dodo yawning. 'Time for beddie-byes, don't you think?'

Holly fled from the window and flung herself face down on her bed. Tears soaked the pillow and her stomach ached from deep stifled sobs.

So Mummy does think it was my fault, she told herself. *She doesn't want me. She just wants my little brother. I will have to behave just the same. Just the same . . . I will have to pretend I don't know . . . until I'm grown up and then . . . and then . . . I'll run away . . . for ever . . .*

Then Hugo was beside her.

'Was it a bad dream?' he asked. 'Don't cry. Don't cry.'

'She doesn't love me,' whispered Holly. 'She doesn't want me. I want Daddy, but he's in India. I don't know how to get to India . . . I want my daddy.'

The words poured brokenly into the pillow.

Hugo lay down beside her and took her hand.

'Listen,' he said. 'My mother has gone on a journey now, but one day she will come and get me and we will go home and you will come with us. My mother will come, I know

159

she will . . . and my father . . . and we take you with us . . .
we will all go to the mountains to the snow and I will teach
you to ski . . . my mother will come . . . we will go home . . .
you will come with us . . . mountains . . .'

He said it all over and over again, a lullaby, until they fell
asleep in the hot late night on the wet pillow.

'Well, well!' said Dodo softly from the doorway. 'How too
sweet. Come and look at this, darling! Proper little Babes in
the Wood.'

'Oh, God!' hissed Kitty. 'We can't leave them like that!'

She pushed past Dodo and carried Hugo back to his
own bed.

She saw the open window, its nearness and wondered
anxiously: how much had they heard? And out of her fear
sprang an unreasonable anger against Hugo. He would pay
for this.

26
The telegram

Hereward was waiting for her at the station with the old school van, a Hereward so stricken that he blurted out in front of the children, 'Thank God you're back! A . . . a telegram came this morning. It's Miles . . . killed on active service . . . convoy was torpedoed . . . his ship went down with all hands . . .'

'Oh no!' Kitty cried. 'No!'

'I've sent for Connie, of course. She's on her way,' said Hereward.

They drove home in grim silence, all staring straight ahead, cut off from one another.

Still in a daze from the night before, Holly felt nothing until she saw her beloved grandmother lying back in a huge armchair, like a broken doll with splayed out legs.

'I'm so cold,' Phoebe kept saying over and over again. 'So cold . . .'

She was clutching the telegram.

The children stared, like forgotten bystanders at a terrible accident.

'Ah, there you are, dears,' Phoebe murmured eventually. 'I'm so cold and there's no tea made . . .'

'Tea! Tea!' said Kitty and Hereward both at once. 'Of course, tea!'

And they bustled away with relief to the cavernous kitchen.

'Come, children, come!'

Phoebe held out her arms.

Holly moved forward and touched Phoebe's hand.

'Oh, Grandmamma, you do feel cold. Oh, poor Grandmamma!' And she slipped gently on to Phoebe's lap and put her arms round her.

Hugo was standing by the chair and said shyly, but firmly, 'Mrs Nash, the sun will make you warm. The sun.'

He raised his voice and pointed to the window. 'Out there it is still so hot. Come to the little house on wheels and I will turn you to the sun.'

'Good fellow!' cried Hereward, who was hovering in the doorway wondering why he had never noticed before how long it takes a kettle to boil.

'Come, Phoebe! Go with the children, my dear, and we will bring you tea.'

Obediently Phoebe went with the children.

Holly took her by the hand, and Hugo ran ahead, eyeing

the sky. He turned the summer house into the warming, blinding sun rays so they would sink into the bones and shut out all pain.

Holly guided Phoebe on to the cushioned hammock and set it rocking, gently rocking, and when her silent tears began to fall Hugo found the clean handkerchief Kitty had given him that morning and Holly tried to wipe them away.

Connie arrived next morning, bringing Imogen with her.

'You kids must go off somewhere and play,' Kitty said to the three subdued children. 'I've made you some sandwiches. You can go to the village and get some fizzy lemonade and have a picnic somewhere . . .'

'He was wrong,' said Imogen angrily, as they trudged down the drive to the village.

'Wrong, what about?' asked Holly.

'He said "*Au revoir*",' said Imogen. 'But he was wrong. We never did see him again . . .'

She was rubbing at her eyes, trying to stop the tears before they came out.

But Hugo could not cry.

He was shattered not only by this family's grief but by his own: his parents gone and no more Red Cross messages, and now . . . Mr Nash who had taken him away from them so he could be safe . . . Mr Nash . . . dead?

'Poor everybody,' said Holly in a shaky little voice.

'Damn this bloody war!' Imogen shouted suddenly. 'Damn it!'

'Yes!' Holly added, 'Damn, blast and hell!'

And they all began shouting, 'Damn this war! Bloody war ... Damn Hitler,' until they saw the vicar coming towards them on his bicycle. If he had heard them he gave no sign.

'Going somewhere nice?' he asked, slowing down. 'Good idea! It helps to keep busy at times like these. I'm just going to look in on the rest of the family. Have fun!' And he went on his way.

'We're being followed,' Imogen said, when they were coming out of the shop with the lemonade. 'Don't look, but some village boys are following us – they're carrying some of those big bulrushes. Quick! Into the woods!'

They scurried across the green into the beech woods, but one quick look round showed them they were still being followed by four or five big boys now, wielding the long bulrushes like spears.

'They'll beat us up if they catch us!' said Imogen. 'We better hide!'

And they plunged further into the woods till they came to a huge old tree with a great mossy hollow in its trunk.

'In here!' whispered Imogen, going first and crouching down to make room for the others. Hugo and Holly were piling in on top of her when there was a sudden angry buzzing noise right on top of them and Imogen leapt up with a dreadful shriek.

'Ow! Ow! Ow! I've been stung! I've been stung! Let me out! Let me get out!'

And she pushed past the others, still yelling and screaming.

She had sat in a wasps' nest, and now all three of them were being stung.

The children ran from the tree as fast as their legs would carry them and headed home blindly. The little gang of boys watched them, laughing cruelly, and fell on the abandoned picnic as soon as Imogen, Holly and Hugo were out of sight.

Their cries and groans brought Kitty and Connie out of the drawing-room where they had been sitting with Phoebe and Hereward. With a mixture of sympathy and exasperation they dabbed at the stings with vinegar and ice cubes from the ancient refrigerator.

'And now go over to the other house,' ordered Kitty, 'and have a rest, listen to the gramophone, or play *Snap* or something to take your minds off the pain. We simply can't have you disturbing the grandparents today!'

Over at the butler's house Imogen the tomboy made an incredible fuss. She buried herself in the sofa cushions and told Holly to draw the curtains.

'Honestly!' said Holly. 'Anyone would think you were the only one to get stung!'

'I got the worst of it, I know I did, I know I did!' Imogen moaned.

Holly and Hugo retreated to the kitchen with the cards and tried not to exchange smiles at the background of groans as they played *Snap* rather slowly in a haze of pain.

In the days that followed a terrible silence fell over Marlowes – silence about the death of Miles. Phoebe put herself to bed and closed her door on them all. Hereward was nowhere to be seen. Connie and Imogen went home. Kitty took to cleaning out all the cupboards. She snapped at the children whenever they appeared, so they kept out of her way, only coming in at meal times.

After a week Phoebe rose up dry-eyed. She too busied herself with arranging the flowers, dead-heading the roses, digging out buttercups and dandelions. Sometimes she could be heard talking to herself, but no one dared draw close enough to hear what she was saying. She took up her knitting needles and taught Kitty how to turn the heel of a sock. When they were tired of knitting khaki socks, khaki balaclavas and khaki mittens they turned to embroidering war slogans. Kitty chose BETTER POT LUCK WITH CHURCHILL TODAY THAN HUMBLE PIE WITH HITLER TOMORROW. She even managed to sew a recognisable casserole and a passable pie dish in lazy daisy stitch.

And while they knitted or sewed, they listened to the news on the wireless. Four times a day they listened to the news, jabbing their needles rapidly in and out of wool and cloth.

27

Separated

It was Connie who unknowingly brought about the separation of Holly and Hugo.

She came on one of her flying visits, bearing gifts.

'I've brought you some saved-up sugar rations,' she said. 'Thought you could do with it with two children in the house. And I've brought a copy of the *Just So Stories* for Hugo ... something to keep him amused and help his English. Kids can be such a nuisance when they're bored, can't they?'

Kitty was glad of the sugar, but the mention of Hugo niggled, reminding her of some thought she had mislaid about him.

They were in Lady Marlowe's sitting-room with Phoebe, who was happily fussing over tea things.

Kitty joined Connie at the window.

Robert Pendleton was walking slowly down the drive, Hugo at his side, crow-like and gawky in his navy-blue gabardine raincoat, bare knees gnarled between grey shorts and grey stockings. Holly was running ahead of them, then back to them in uneven circles like a happy puppy dog fetching invisible sticks.

'Hasn't he grown?' said Connie. 'He's going to be tall and very good-looking.'

'Good-looking?' echoed Kitty.

'Mm,' said Connie. 'Give him another ten years and he'll be breaking hearts. How old is he now?'

'He was ten in October,' said Kitty stiffly. 'He's six months older than Holly.'

At that moment Holly danced to Hugo's side. Her plaits were flying. She was talking animatedly. Robert and Hugo were laughing. Holly, it seemed, had said something funny. Kitty could see her sunny face: a happy girl taking a walk with friends.

And then Kitty saw again the two children fast asleep on one small bed under the eaves of Dodo's hot little house. Heard again Dodo's slurred voice in her ear, 'Proper little Babes in the Wood!' And remembered at last that she'd been going to talk to Hereward about this as soon as they got home.

'Holly will be ten soon,' she muttered. 'She's always mooching about after him. Oh, God! I can't have that!'

'Have what?' snapped Connie. 'Oh, don't be silly, Kitty! We're talking about a little boy and a little girl. Anyway I'm all for kids growing up together naturally.'

'I know you are,' sneered Kitty, thinking disapprovingly of Imogen's co-ed schooling. 'But I found them in bed together one night last summer.'

'Oh dear!' cried Phoebe, putting her hands up to her cheeks.

'What do you mean exactly by in bed together?' asked Connie.

'Lying in each other's arms,' said Kitty untruthfully.

'Were they . . . were they . . . sharing a room?' gasped Phoebe.

'Yes, Mamma,' said Kitty. 'The house was tiny and as Connie has just said, they are only children and it was only for the one night.'

'Oh dear!' breathed Phoebe.

'Oh come on, you two!' said Connie impatiently. 'Perhaps they'd been telling each other stories . . . or . . . or one of them had had a bad dream or something.'

'Perhaps,' agreed Kitty. 'Come to think of it, Holly did rather look as if she'd been crying.'

'I wonder why,' said Connie.

'How should I know?' snapped Kitty. 'Anyway, it worried me – even if it was innocent. I feel they spend too much time together and they are growing up fast. In fact it worried me so much I was going to tell Hereward all about it when we got home, but when he met us . . . met us with the news of Miles . . . it went right out of my head.'

'Of course, dear, of course,' murmured Phoebe. 'But you

170

were quite right to be troubled and something must be done. They've been happy little playfellows, but perhaps from now on he should spend his holidays with other boys.'

'Oh, Mother, Mother!' sighed Connie.

'Why not, dear?' said Phoebe brightly. 'What about the vicar?'

'What about the vicar?'

'He's got four sons,' explained Kitty.

'But you can't do that to the poor kid!' cried Connie. 'All term with boys. All his hols with hearty little rugger players! I wonder what Miles would have felt about that?'

'Miles,' Phoebe repeated tremulously. 'Yes, we must think what Miles would have wanted for his little refugee. After all, Hugo is in a sense a symbol of all we are fighting for.'

'Of course,' said Kitty. 'Miles would want what is best for Hugo.'

'Well,' challenged Connie. 'What is best for him?'

'Surely to fit in,' said Phoebe. 'So he need never feel an outsider.'

'You mean to be absorbed into your imperial, Christian world?' said Connie.

'Well, darling, of course he should not be allowed to forget his own world.'

'Was he brought up religious?' Connie asked. 'Has anybody thought to ask him? Well, never mind. Even if he wasn't there must be so many other things he misses – we wouldn't even know what – attitudes, atmosphere. For all we know he may be starved for hugs and kisses – and jokes we don't know, let alone understand the humour of. I bet he wasn't always such a solemn little boy . . . and I bet he misses *Kuglhupf* and *goulash* and caraway soup.'

'Kugl . . . what? Caraway soup?' Phoebe muttered. 'And what about Hebrew?'

'Quite,' said Connie. 'We-ell, if you both really think it is necessary to part the poor little things, then your vicar sounds like the best hope . . .'

'That's it then!' said Phoebe, spooning tea into the pot. 'I'll ask Hereward to talk to the Fullers as soon as possible . . . the Fullers are unusual,' she added. 'They lived in India for many years, you know . . . met Mr Gandhi, I believe . . . sometimes I feel Mr Fuller's heart isn't in the militant hymns he feels it is his duty to make us sing . . .'

But later, the night before Hugo left for the vicarage, Phoebe had second thoughts.

As she sat in front of her triple mirrors, flashing her silver brush through her hair, she saw Hugo and Holly. In her mirrors, she saw them running towards her, lost and scared, clutching crushed cowslips; leaning against her on that first day in the rose garden; lying on the sunbaked stone while she read to them after the fête – and Hugo had said . . . what had he said? 'Where are the mothers?' And later Holly leading her towards the summer house – how cold she had

172

been – and helping her to sit there while Hugo turned her into the sun.

She put down her brush and said out loud, 'Hugo and Holly will be all right, won't they, Hereward?'

'Of course they will,' said Hereward.

28
Doodlebug

Holly missed Hugo very much, and hoped when Easter came at least to see him in church. She did not know that the Reverend Fuller had sent him out into the garden to draw the apple tree, and watch over his younger sons tumbling about in a wigwam made from old blankets and a clothes rack.

'It's not fair,' his older boys had moaned, as, scrubbed and brushed, they walked to church on Easter Sunday.

'Would you think it fair,' said their father, 'to be asked to rejoice in a belief you didn't share? The Jews are still waiting for the Messiah.'

His sons stared at him.

'We-ell,' said their father kindly. 'Something to think about during my sermon!'

Over lunch in the vicarage Hugo learned about Passover, when the Angel of Death passed the Jews by, and Moses led them out of Egypt into the wilderness. He learned about

Seder and candles; about the blood of the lamb and bitter herbs. And about Elijah's goblet, always filled and waiting for him.

'Elijah,' said Mr Fuller, 'was a great and wise being, so special it is told that when it was time for him to die a chariot of fire appeared and horses of fire and he "went up by a whirlwind into heaven." '

'Enough for one day!' Mrs Fuller then said and dished out sweets saved from her ration to all the boys. 'Now take Hugo up to the Hornby set and show him all the doings.'

There was a whole room at the top of the huge, Victorian house, given over to a model railway, tracks curving round papier-mâché hills, covered in bushes, little figures and toy animals.

There were stations too with milk churns and mailbags.

'We've taken down the names, though,' said one of the boys, 'just like on the real stations, so the Germans won't know where they are, when, if, they ever get here, that is.'

'Of course,' said his brother, 'we all know who spends more time than anyone up here when there's no one looking!'

'Who?' asked Hugo.

'Our mother!' they all carolled. 'She says it's her way of letting off steam – ugh! What a pun! Ugh!'

Hugo was very happy with the Fullers. They taught him to play croquet and a card game called *Cheat*. He went with them to Wales and climbed the paths of Snowdonia. He spent patient hours training their pet white mouse to walk a tightrope made out of a dressing-gown cord. He even rigged up a safety net made from an old string shopping bag. He persuaded Mrs Fuller to part with a precious lump of Cheddar cheese to tempt the mouse across the rope. 'After all,' he said with his shy smile, 'the cheese is called "mouse trap"!'

Mr Fuller led him through the Old Testament, picking out the great stories, the poetry, the prophecies and taught him to write the Hebrew alphabet with Indian ink and pen on good paper hoarded from before the war.

At night Hugo would fish out his little notebook from under his pillow and add to the growing list of things to tell Holly and, one day, to his mother and father.

Rumours began to fly, which proved to be true, that Hitler had a new and deadly weapon up his sleeve – a pilotless plane which was actually a bomb, set on course for London and other big cities. When its sinister deep slow growling turned to a splutter and the flames in its tail went out, the short silence which followed was a terrifying warning that this 'doodlebug' or 'buzz bomb' was going to explode immediately. So in the school holidays Connie sent Imogen to stay with Kitty and Holly.

Holly missed Hugo and was in no mood to put up with Imogen's sharp tongue and bossy ways. But, perhaps because she had Holly to herself, Imogen was much nicer than she used to be.

The two girls spent rather a lot of time lying around on their beds, eating stale chocolate from South Africa, while Imogen, as she had promised long ago, graphically described to Holly how babies were made.

'I'm never going to let that happen to me!' Imogen would say, half angrily, half tearfully.

Phoebe tried to read them *The Pilgrim's Progress* in the summer house. But they fidgeted so much she gave up and let them loll about on the grass, making daisy chains, and did not stop them from reading *Jane Eyre* out loud to each other, smiling as she watched them both fall passionately in love with Mr Rochester.

Kitty, however, did not approve.

'You girls are altogether spending far to much time loafing about!' she would say. 'Go on! Up you get and go for a good long walk before lunch!'

'Have you noticed,' said Imogen one day as they set off at an obedient trot down the back drive, a trot which dwindled to a dawdle once out of Kitty's sight, 'have you noticed that the door into the kitchen garden isn't locked?'

They went in and ate Lord Marlowe's nectarines.

When the loss was reported by the ever-watchful ancient gardener, they were sent to bed without supper and grew more friendly toward each other than they ever had before.

One day, when they were sitting on the stone lions guarding the empty fountain, Lord Marlowe himself waved to them as he dashed from the house to a waiting car. He had been to raid his cellar for wine. He was in Navy uniform, set off by a long white scarf.

'Of course,' said Imogen, waving back, 'Mr Rochester wasn't as handsome as Lord Marlowe, but he had a sort of dark, wild . . . wild . . .'

'Glory?' suggested Holly.

'Yes!' breathed Imogen. 'Glory.'

She sat there swinging her legs.

'I've been thinking,' she suddenly said. 'I expect making a baby is all right if the two people love each other.'

Holly decided that perhaps Imogen wasn't so bad after all, and for the first time she was really sorry when it was time for her to go home.

The doodlebug landed just before dawn.

That night Holly had been sleeping in her father's half of the mahogany twin beds. From time to time Kitty allowed her this as a treat.

Holly was awake, listening out for the rats she was sure lived in the ceiling, wishing Imogen was still there to re-assure her that they couldn't get out.

When Kitty heard the approaching rasp of the flying bomb, she grabbed the torch she always kept on the bedside table and lay there, rigid, terrified, listening.

'Go on!' she commanded silently. 'Don't stop here . . . go on . . . not here . . . somewhere else . . .'

But the self-propelled monstrous thing exploded in the woods a quarter of mile from the butler's house.

All the windows blew out and the ceilings fell down, large pieces of plaster miraculously just missing Kitty and Holly, crashing around them to the floor, leaving a huge space above them, shaped like a map of some unknown country.

Holly stared at her immobile mother, arms stiffly at her sides, covered now in thick white plaster dust.

'Mummy!' she croaked. 'Mummy! You look like a dead person!'

'Shut up!' said Kitty. And then jumped up and out of her skin as a ghostly voice floated up to them through the glassless windows.

'K-i-t-t-y? A-r-e y-o-u a-l-l r-i-g-h-t?'

It was Hereward on air-raid duty that night.

For the second time, Kitty and Holly spent a night in the famous Red Room.

'At the last minute!' Phoebe cried indignantly. 'They come up with this new evil device!'

'The war isn't over yet,' said Hereward soberly. 'They'll go down fighting. And God alone knows what else they may have up their sleeves.'

'It can't be long now,' protested Phoebe. 'It can't be, and I want Hugo here with us again. I'd never forgive myself,' she added irrationally, 'if he was bombed out in another family's house.'

They all walked up later to see where the bomb had landed, but they were not allowed anywhere near it. They were stopped by a member of the Home Guard.

'This one took the wrong road for London,' he said. 'But if you want to see the force of the blast go and take a look over there.' They followed his directions to the far side of the woods; stood and stared silently at the shards of treetrunks, ripped to shreds like tattered flesh, stripped bare of all their bark, all the leaves fallen to the ground as if autumn had come too soon; stared and winced at the murder of the wood, the sawdust everywhere, what branches there were hanging loose, like the shattered limbs of grotesque marionettes: a copse of shattered beeches – blitzed, broken, dead.

29

The newsreel

The war was drawing to its end.

Phoebe, Hereward and Kitty listened to all the news bulletins, and one bright summer morning Holly picked up the words: 'D-day! D-day! We've landed on the beaches of Normandy!'

'France, darling! France!' Phoebe explained to Holly. 'We're liberating France!'

'It'll all be over by Christmas, surely?' said Kitty.

'That's what we always say,' sighed Hereward. 'No, my dears, the war will not be over until we have crossed the Rhine into Germany itself.'

As if to hurry things along, when gliders laden with paratroopers filled the sky, flying low, hour after hour over Marlowes, Kitty spread her wet washing into V for Victory shapes on the grass.

But the enemy did not give up that easily: a new kind of rocket began to drop on England, giving no warning of any kind and killing thousands. Autumn leaves had fallen, the frosts returned and the daffodils were out again before the Rhine was crossed and Kitty decided on a trip to London.

'I think we can risk it,' she said to Holly gaily. 'The Germans are now really on the run. They won't sling anything at us now. And you need new summer dresses for school.'

'Can Hugo come?' asked Holly.

'Of course,' said Kitty. She presumed that someone soon would be coming to take him away for good.

The summer dresses were quickly tried on and quickly paid for and there was time for a visit to Mme Tussaud's. The children had been once before and made a beeline for their favourite waxwork figures. Hugo's were the little princes in the Tower. He could not believe that they were dead; not dead, just sleeping, very pale, but just sleeping. Holly ran first to Sleeping Beauty. She was fascinated by the rise and fall of her breathing. How sweet she looked, like Snow White in her glass coffin, sweet and peaceful waiting for her prince's kiss.

From there they ran to the mirrors whose curves and distortions produced the funniest and scariest foreshortenings of their legs, bodies and faces. They left the waxworks laughing, relieved to see that they were neither dwarfs nor giants.

'Well,' said Kitty, 'we've got time to kill before our train. Shall we go to the news cinema and see the cartoons? A last wartime treat, who knows?'

They saw Pluto and Goofy and Donald Duck in bright technicolour.

Then came music in a major key, and the crowing cock – white against black – of Pathé News.

In a steady, clipped voice the newsreader said, 'Belsen'. Said, 'Horrors,' said, 'atrocities,' said, 'torture,' said, 'furnaces, ovens, smoking chimneys, ash, mass graves, electrified wire.' Said, 'agonised deaths of hundreds and thousands of prisoners . . .'

Kitty said, 'Don't look!' Hissed, 'Don't look! Hide your eyes!'

But it was too late.

They had looked.

And, because she had said not to, they went on looking. Yes, they covered their eyes with their hands, but peeped through fingers at the living skeletons. Some were moving in the slowest of slow motion, but mostly they were lying on the ground, a few smiling weakly, all staring, staring with their huge hollow eyes, skulls shaven, their bones draped in striped pyjamas far too large. And close by corpses . . . heap upon heap, lying often naked or in rags, spread-eagled like broken marionettes.

No one in the cinema stirred or fled.

No one cried out.

Belsen. Belsen. Belsen.

The newsreader drummed away at the hideous word until its tocsin roused Kitty at last into action.

'Come on, you two. Let's get out of here,' she snapped, 'or we'll miss the train.'

She hustled them out and in the bright light of the foyer, to her surprise and relief, bumped into Robert Pendleton.

'That was unfortunate,' he murmured, keeping an eye watchfully on the two children who had gone straight out into the street.

'I told them not to look,' she said. 'I told them . . .'

'I'm not blaming you,' he said. 'No one could have known . . .'

He took her by the arm and, catching up with the children, escorted them into the station and on to their train.

Smoke belched past the carriage window.

'I've got a headache,' said Holly, very pale.

'So have I,' said Kitty. 'Come here, darling,' she said, drawing her daughter close to her and stroking her forehead. 'You didn't eat enough lunch . . . that's probably why you've got a headache.'

But both knew that was not the real reason.

Cradled by her mother, the rhyme *Who Killed Cock Robin* floated into Holly's head, but instead of 'Who saw him die?' she realised she was hearing, 'Who saw them die? I saw them die . . .'

She looked at her mother's ashen face. She looked at Hugo sitting opposite her. His eyes were closed. She knew what he was thinking about.

'Well!' said Robert Pendleton a little too heartily. 'I've

been up to London to see my old mother. She's been living in her flat bang in the centre of London all through the war! Wouldn't even go down to the air-raid shelters! "No German is going to get me out of my nice bed!" is what she said! But what have you been doing in London today?'

'We went to the waxworks,' said Holly, 'and I got new summer dresses for school!'

'Did you, by Jove?' said Robert. 'Come to think of it you have shot up a bit, haven't you?'

'Do you think Daddy will recognise me?'

'Of course he will! And besides you've still got the same sweet face. Any more news of when he might be back?'

'He's hoping in a month or two,' said Kitty. 'Possibly sooner.'

'It'll be good to have him back again,' said Robert.

Holly smiled at him warmly.

Then Hugo spoke.

'Please, sir,' he said. 'I have still one bird to finish for my mother. It is difficult, this one . . . the wing . . . the last wing. Would you have some time to help me?'

'Of course,' said Robert. 'All the time in the world now it's the hols. We could set ourselves up out-of-doors if this weather keeps up . . . let the real birds inspire us, but I've just had a bright idea! How about coming to tea with me in Woodham and letting poor Mrs Nash go on home and have a bit of a rest? I know a jolly good place where they have home-made cakes and sometimes fresh boiled eggs and toast!'

'Oh yes!' said Holly. 'Shall we Hugo, shall we?'

'Yes please,' agreed Hugo. 'I am very hungry.'

'You're always very hungry!' said Holly. 'Mummy thinks you've got hollow legs!' And somehow they all managed to laugh.

On the back drive Kitty saw Phoebe coming towards her, and she began to cry.

'Oh, Mamma!' she sobbed and, babbling incoherently, flung herself into Phoebe's arms.

'Kitty! Kitty!' soothed Phoebe. 'What is it? What is it? And where are the children?'

'With Robert. In Woodham,' said Kitty. 'Oh, Mamma, I've seen such things . . . we've seen such things . . . ovens, Mamma! Ovens! And thousands starved to death. This filthy, filthy war . . . we've all been playing a game . . . as if war was an exciting chessboard! Well, this afternoon I've seen the pawns. Nothing, nothing will ever be the same again. And that poor boy, that poor little Hugo . . . and my Holly . . . my precious child. Oh, I'm sorry, Mamma . . . I've got such a terrible headache . . . I must go and lie down. Talk to Robert later – when the children aren't there!'

She tore herself out of Phoebe's arms, rushed into the butler's house, up the stairs, into her room and flung herself on to the bed.

Distressed and puzzled, Phoebe stared up at Kitty's window. *Poor girl*, she thought, *she was* very *upset – not like her at all. Ah well, Robert will explain. It surely can't be anything too terrible.*

It was only as she reached her own door that she wondered if she had heard right: Kitty's choked voice in her ear. 'Ovens, Mamma! Ovens . . .'

'I can't have heard right,' said Phoebe. 'It's not possible!'

30
The dark wood

When the war ended a few weeks later, and with Hitler dead by his own hand in a bunker in Berlin, there was a public holiday. For the first time in six long years the church bells peeled out again and a bonfire was built on the village green.

'You must wear your best dress,' said Kitty to Holly. 'And Hugo must wear a jacket and tie.'

'Oh no!' groaned Holly. Her best dress had long sleeves and was made of thick velvet. 'It's a winter dress and it's boiling today! It's not fair, Mummy, you're wearing a summer dress, so why can't I?'

'Do as you're told,' her mother ordered.

When the house-high bonfire was lit and roaring Kitty pushed the children forward.

'Go on!' she urged. 'Enjoy yourselves! This is a day to remember – something to tell your children about!'

And she went off to help the other women with the party food and drink.

'Holly! Holly! Hello!' cried a familiar voice.

It was Gillian from school, and behind her, Jennifer and all her family.

'Well,' Gillian smiled. 'We won in the end, didn't we? I'm spending the day with the "Mop End Kids".'

'When are you coming to visit us?' Jennifer's mother asked. 'I hear you and your friend have got bicycles? Perhaps now the war is over you will be allowed to ride over and visit us?'

'Oh yes, please!' breathed Holly. I'll go and ask Mummy! But first, have you still got your mice, Sissi and Piffi? Because Hugo knows a jolly good way to teach them to walk the tightrope!'

'Really?' said Jennifer. 'I'd like to see that, wouldn't you, Gillian? Oh you must come soon! Can they come soon, Mummy?'

And murmuring friendly promises they all went in search of Kitty.

All except Hugo, who slipped away from them and the sweltering fire and crept into the dark wood.

His bladder was bursting from all the lemonade he had drunk. He was sweating in his grey flannels. He had a headache from the church bells' clapping tongues.

Brushing against branches and hanging stick insects, he pushed on, seeking silence and coolness. He emptied his bladder and loosened his tie. Only then did he see how far he had come.

The camp! He'd come nearly as far as the camp, which had been used last year by the Americans who had come to help liberate France. He could see the camouflaged tents beyond the high barbed-wire fence. The images he had seen in the news cinema flashed before him. Suddenly he felt shivery in the warm, still air. He began to step backwards the way he had come. Then he heard a low whistle and jumped edgily.

A skinny, shaven man in grey was grinning at him through the fence, smiling and beckoning. Hugo stayed where he was, clasping a young treetrunk, but curious enough not to run away.

'OK, OK, little boy!' said the man in a thick accent.

He grinned and pointed. '*Domoi*! Home! Soon I go that way . . . home! *Da*! Yes! *Domoi*! Thank you kind British people, but I go home . . . *Ukrainia* . . . Ukraine, yes?'

'Ohh!' stammered Hugo. 'Yes. Good. Good.'

He had chocolate in his pocket. Phoebe had given it to him. 'Victory rations', she'd called it, hoarded since the Americans had swept through the village, grinding up the tarmac with their enormous, starred tanks, cutting corners in their jeeps, handing out what they called "candy" wherever they went.

Hugo took the chocolate out of his pocket, melting in its silver wrapper, and approached the fence shyly.

'Here,' he offered. 'For you.'

The man snatched the chocolate and hid it in the folds of his jacket. He patted the secret place.

'*Spassivo*! Thank you, little boy. This your home? Is nice place, but not my place . . .'

'I must go now,' said Hugo, pointing the way back to the village green.

'OK, OK! You go now and I go soon, eh?' The man grinned broadly and gave him the thumbs-up sign followed by the Victory salute. 'Good boy. All good now, OK?'

No, thought Hugo, as he stumbled back to the bonfire. Not all good now. When am I going home? Have I still got a home?

'Ah, there you are!' said Phoebe, who was clapping her hands to encourage Mr Fuller as he struggled with a wheezy accordion. 'Holly needs you as a dancing partner!'

'Please, Mrs Nash,' said Hugo. 'When am I going home?'

'Soon, dear,' said Phoebe distractedly. 'I am sure it will be soon. Now off you go and join in the dancing!'

But Hugo heard his mother's voice whispering, 'Soon . . . soon we will all be together again.'

It had not been soon. And they still had not come and, in his heart of hearts he had known for a long time now that they would not be coming . . .

Again he asked, 'Sorry, Mrs Nash, please, sorry, but when am I going home?' not daring to ask outright, 'What will happen to me now? Where will I go?'

'Soon, dear,' said Phoebe rather impatiently this time. 'I said soon, didn't I? Now, off you go, dear, and join in the fun.'

But Hugo stood mute and close at her side. She looked down at him. She really did not want to be reminded today of suffering, not Hugo's, or her own, let alone Robert Pendleton's dreadful account of that terrible newsreel.

'Don't worry, Hugo,' she managed to say. 'We will make enquiries as soon as the holiday is over. Now do go and dance with Holly, there's a good boy, or she'll feel left out.'

31

Homecoming

Holly made a special little calendar on which she crossed off the days till her father's return.

And indeed the first hours of Guy's homecoming were sweet: he hugged Holly tightly and smiled with pleasure at the poster she had painted and pinned over the door: *Vive mon père*, it said: long live my father; at Kitty in her prettiest dress; at the table laid with a starched cloth and shining silver; at the feast of chicken from the farm up the road with a heap of new potatoes and peas from the kitchen garden. He had brought beautiful presents from India – a long silk scarf for Kitty and a set of elephants carved out of ivory for Holly.

It was not long, however, before he seemed to find fault with nearly everything.

'Surely the child should be in bed by now?' he said on that first evening.

'It's only half past six!' Kitty said. 'Holly's not a baby any more!'

'Can't she hear the wrong note?' Holly heard him say when she was practising her minuet to be able to play to him. 'That's a B flat she keeps playing instead of B natural.'

And he strode across to the piano and barked at her, 'Practice is about correcting mistakes, Holly, not just playing the same bit over and over again wrong!'

Holly was nearly in tears and jumped up and ran from the room.

'Don't be so touchy!' her father called after her.

She soon realised that neither she nor her mother would ever be able to explain anything of their life to this strict stranger with a ramrod spine.

And then, for a moment, the father who had played with her, had secrets with her, would appear briefly, leaving Holly puzzled and bewildered.

Sometimes he had breakfast in bed.

'You deserve to be spoiled a little longer,' Kitty said.

Holly would take the tray up, the newspaper tucked under her arm.

One morning, struggling with the bedroom doorknob, Holly dropped the paper.

'Damn,' she said.

Her father was sitting up in bed, looking very serious.

'Thank you, darling,' he said to Holly. He took the tray on to his knees and began tapping at his egg.

He cleared his throat and said, 'Did I hear you say "Damn" at the door?'

'Yes, Daddy.'

'I don't like to think of my little girl swearing. Don't let it happen again.'

'No, Daddy. I'm very sorry,' said Holly.

Her father smiled at her forgivingly, so that as she moved towards the door, Holly found the courage to turn and ask, 'Daddy, d-d-did you kill anyone in the war?'

She saw her father's face soften and yet fill with pain as he answered in the voice she knew from long ago: 'No, my darling, no, I didn't kill anyone . . .'

They looked at one another in deep, relieved silence.

Then Holly ran downstairs with the same joyful heart she had had when she ran to hug him on the day he came home.

But her heart sank again the day she heard her parents arguing about Hugo.

'He always used to spend the holidays with us!' her mother was saying. 'I told you that in my letters! Until he went to the vicar's family, but Phoebe insisted he should return to us after the doodlebug and that terrible newsreel. Felt we'd imposed on the vicar long enough and that Hugo was our responsibility and should be with us all, so I'm expecting him back here now term's ended. He won't be here much longer, anyway – I told you Connie's in touch with the Red Cross . . . no, your mother can't look after him! She's got enough to do getting ready to move back to Swanstown. I'm sorry, darling, but he must come over here until he leaves.'

'Oh, very well,' Holly heard her father say at last.

He did not sound at all enthusiastic, but when he saw Hugo again he tried to be nice to him. Holly wondered if her father was remembering that he had helped to save Hugo's life.

Hugo felt as shy and uncomfortable with Guy Nash as Guy felt with Hugo.

'Enjoyed yourself here have you, Altman?' Guy asked over the lunch table one day.

'Yes, sir,' said Hugo.

'Learned to play cricket?'

'Yes, sir.'

'Good. Good. Remember Prague, do you?'

'Yes, sir.'

'Beautiful city. Wish I'd had time to see more of it.'

'Yes, sir.'

Hugo went on bravely, 'Sir, I am very sorry about the other Mr Nash . . .'

'Yes,' said Guy gruffly. 'We all are . . .' He paused and then said, 'But life goes on, you know! I hear you're doing a spot of woodwork with Mr Pendleton? Carving something. Is that right?'

'Birds, sir. I'm carving birds.'

'Birds?' Guy nearly choked on his lettuce leaves.

'For my mother, sir.'

'Oh. Likes that sort of thing, does she?'

'I hope so, sir.'

'I'm sure she will,' said Guy. 'Mothers generally like that sort of thing. Come to think of it, I made a stool for my mother when I was a boy at The Priory and I'm pretty sure she still uses it.'

'Hugo won a prize at school, you know, Daddy!' Holly interrupted.

'Did he, by Jove!' said Guy. 'What for?'

'Per-per-sever-ance, sir,' said Hugo.

'Good show!' said Guy. 'Good show!'

'And Hugo paints lovely pictures,' said Holly.

'Does he?' said Guy. 'Nice hobby, all that sort of thing. But what are you going to do when you grow up?'

'I don't know yet, sir,' lied Hugo. Even Holly didn't know that he planned to paint a ceiling like Michelangelo, but his would show Elijah being carried up into heaven in the fiery chariot in the whirlwind.

Hugo's quiet manner and solemn eyes were making Guy uneasy.

What an unruly mop of curls, he said to himself.

'You need a haircut, Altman!' he announced.

'Yes, sir,' said Hugo obediently.

32

'The news is grim'

A few days later Connie appeared.

'The news is grim,' she said, ushering her parents and Guy into the sitting-room and shutting the door. 'In fact it's terrible. I've sent Imogen off to play with Holly and told her to keep her mouth shut. Oh, God!' She paused, near to tears. 'Where's Hugo?'

'It's all right,' said Phoebe. 'I saw him ages ago trotting off to Robert's room.'

'We need a family council,' said Connie. 'Where's Kitty?'

'Gone to have her hair done,' said Guy.

'Oh well, never mind. I don't think this can wait,' said Connie, pulling some papers from her bag. 'This is the information I got from the Red Cross. Apparently Hugo's parents were taken away – in 1941 – to Theresienstadt – not far from Prague . . . a sort of transit camp,' she added in answer to the silent question on everyone's faces. 'And it is now known that from there the Nazis deported everyone to the concentration camps . . . mostly to the gas chambers at Auschwitz – in Poland.'

'Oh!' gasped Phoebe.

Ever since Robert had explained to her about the Belsen newsreel and confirmed that Kitty might well have been choking on the words "ovens", she had feared this day must come, that the hideous skeletal names of the camps would arrive clanking and brittle in her house.

'Their names are not on the lists of survivors,' said Constance dully. 'The likelihood is that they were gassed at Auschwitz. That's what the man said. So . . . who's going to tell him?'

'I can't,' said Phoebe faintly.

'No, no, Mother!' said Guy. 'Of course you can't. It should be a man, but certainly I don't feel I know him well enough.'

'How about Robert?' said Hereward.

'Robert! Of course!' said Phoebe. 'Hugo loves Robert.'

'Where are they?' asked Guy.

'As a matter of fact, I can see them down on the far lawn under the cedars, carving those blessed birds,' said Hereward.

Phoebe opened her mouth as if to prolong the discussion – anything to delay the terrible moment of sending for their old friend in order to ask him to tell a child that his parents had been murdered.

'Well,' said Guy gruffly, 'best get it over with. I'll go and fetch Robert.'

Connie went and sat on the edge of her mother's chair and put her arm round her.

'Oh,' said Phoebe. 'The poor child. How will he ever get over it?'

'I don't know, Mother,' said Connie sorrowfully. 'I don't know.'

Imogen sat in the pantry on the green baize table, swinging her legs.

She had not been able to keep her mouth shut.

'They went everywhere rounding up all the Jews and putting them in these special camps . . . lots of them have been found now . . . then they gassed them in special rooms . . . or shot them . . . and threw the bodies into ovens, or into pits they had made them dig.'

'I know,' said Holly, who was flipping the lid of a box full of spoons up and down, up and down.

'What?' shrieked Imogen. 'What do you mean – you know?'

'Hugo and I saw it on a newsreel by mistake. It was horrible. They were wearing baggy pyjamas . . . their heads were all shaved . . . some had no clothes on at all . . . there were hundreds of dead ones all piled up.'

'Stop it! Stop it!' cried Imogen, jumping down and covering her ears.

'D-do you th-think Hugo's parents were in one of those camps?' Holly stammered.

'Probably,' said Imogen. She closed her mouth firmly and stared at Holly. She so wanted not to break her promise to her mother, but Holly read the truth at once in Imogen's eyes.

'Oh, no,' whispered Holly. 'Oh, no!' She laid her head on the box and let her tears fall in among the spoons. She did not want to cry her eyes out and sob in front of Imogen. 'Poor Hugo . . . poor Hugo . . .' she muttered, wiping her eyes and looking up again. 'Does he know?'

'Not yet,' said Imogen. 'Connie's talking to the grown-ups.'

'Perhaps . . . perhaps I . . . we . . . should go and look for him.'

'No, Holly,' said Imogen. 'Better leave it to them.'

'But . . . but who's going to look after him now?' trembled Holly.

'There's an aunt,' said Imogen, 'somewhere in France. She wants him to come to her. She's all alone too now. Her husband and son were caught and shot. They had gone into hiding in a village in the mountains. They thought they were safe. She only survived because she had gone deep into the woods that day, looking for food for them, mushrooms, I suppose, or nuts or berries.'

'Oh, poor, poor Hugo,' wailed Holly, 'I don't want him to go. He can't go! I want him to stay with us for ever!'

'So do I,' said Imogen. 'He's become a bit like another cousin, really. Can you imagine not having a father and

201

mother? I can't! I can't even begin to think what I'd do without my mother and father.'

'Don't!' begged Holly. 'I can't imagine anything to do with this at all. Don't let's talk about it any more now.'

The two girls were quiet for a moment.

'I was beastly to you when we were young, wasn't I?' said Imogen.

'Yes,' Holly agreed. 'But it was a long time ago and I bet I asked for it sometimes.'

'Oh, I dunno,' said Imogen generously.

'I'm glad it was you telling me about Hugo.'

'That's all right,' said Imogen. 'You can cry in front of me, you know,' she added. 'I cried, if you want to know . . . when Connie told me on the train coming down.'

'Did you?' said Holly. 'Actually I don't feel like crying at the moment. I feel more like yelling and screaming.' She eyed Lord Marlowe's Crown Derby dinner service – shelf upon shelf of it behind the glass doors of the huge dressers which lined the pantry walls. 'I'd like to smash all those plates . . .'

'Perhaps we'd better get out of here before we both start smashing plates!' said Imogen.

'I wish Mummy was back from the hairdresser's,' sighed Holly.

'She will be soon,' said Imogen. 'C'mon, until she is you can share my mother . . .'

33

The birds

'And this evening I thought we'd collect the girls and go for a row,' Robert Pendleton was saying to Hugo when he heard Guy calling him.

'Back in a minute,' he said cheerfully.

'Right you are, sir,' said Hugo. He was happy now that the last bird was coming free of the knotty chunk of wood which had defeated him for so long. The four finished birds lay on the table nearby.

As long as he was handling the birds he forgot the thoughts he had had coming out of the dark wood on Victory Day.

He looked up briefly. He could see the two men walking down the drive, heads close together. Mr Pendleton's back seemed more bowed than usual.

Suddenly it seemed more urgent than ever to finish the last bird. He clutched it firmly by its smooth head and stubbornly went on with his work.

He heard Robert coming towards him at last.

He did not look up, but when he felt Robert's hand on his shoulder he dropped the bird.

He did not turn round.

He could not turn round.

His hands felt twice as large as usual; his legs and feet felt leaden.

'Hugo,' said Robert Pendleton quietly. And because he had not called him "Altman" in the usual way, Hugo knew what he was going to hear.

He flung up his hands and covered his ears.

'No!' he cried. 'No! No! No!'

'Hugo,' said Robert again.

'No!' shouted Hugo.

Gently Robert pulled the boy's hands away from his face.

'You don't need to tell me. You don't have to say anything. I know. I know.'

He pushed Robert's hands away, scooped up his birds and began to run.

He ran straight to the rose garden and flung the birds as far away from him as he could.

'Too late!' he howled. 'Too late! What a waste! What a waste!'

Vile, dry sobs overcame him.

For a long time he did not hear the silence of the rose garden or smell the fragrance of its flowers. Then, very slowly, he became aware again that the earth was still beneath his feet and the sky above him.

He crept towards the scattered birds and crouched close to the warm paving to gather them up, then scrambled to his feet.

'What shall I do with them?' he asked the emptiness. 'Bury them? Here?'

His eye fell on a large rose. He thought it might be the one Mrs Nash had called *Peace*. He searched around for something to dig with and saw an old spade handle leaning against the wall.

He scrabbled and dug till there was a shallow hole big enough for his five birds.

He stood up straight then, and shut his eyes.

There was a prayer his father had taught him.

'*Shema Ysrael*,' he whispered. '*Hear, O Israel. Shema* . . . *shema* . . .'

He heard someone come up behind him.

It was Phoebe.

'Hugo,' she murmured gently. 'Hugo, dear. Dear, dear boy . . .'

'I can't remember,' he whispered, 'I can't remember the words . . .'

'Never mind,' said Phoebe. 'It doesn't matter, darling. God knows what you are trying to say . . .'

'I buried them,' Hugo told her.

'Buried them?' echoed Phoebe, bewildered.

'Yes, my birds . . . the birds I made for m-m-my m-mother . . . I buried them there . . . by that rose . . .'

'Near *Peace*,' said Phoebe, putting an arm very lightly round him. 'What better place? What better place.'

Hugo leaned against her and said, 'This garden is a good place. You brought Holly and me here sometimes when we were frightened, didn't you?'

'Yes,' said Phoebe. 'Yes, I did.'

'And once you read to us about that other good place by the river . . .'

And at that very moment, like some small miracle, Holly and Imogen appeared and said, 'Come on, Hugo! We're going on the river now.'

Holly and Hugo sat in the stern of the boat.

Robert handed Imogen an oar and the two of them rowed out on to the slow-moving river.

Cradled in the boat, rocked gently by the water, the children were silent, sleepy, sad.

The huge red August sun was setting. Swans sailed proudly past, carrying cargoes of cygnets. Moorhens scuttled across the bows. Rings of bright water betrayed the presence of trout. Cows stared, flicked their tails free of flies and went back to grazing.

'I buried the birds, sir,' said Hugo, as they turned homewards. 'In the rose garden.'

'Of course,' said Robert. 'Of course . . .'

'Would you like a turn with my oar?' Imogen asked Hugo.

'Yes,' said Hugo.

'I didn't know you could row,' said Robert.

'Miles taught him,' said Holly.

'Taught us all,' said Imogen proudly.

Hugo settled into a good rhythm with Robert.

'My . . .' he began, then faltered, 'm-my m-mother . . . f-father they w-will be . . . w-would be glad I learned this in England . . .'

He leaned on his oar and, with Robert's arm round him, Hugo began at last to cry.

That evening, when the children were all in bed, the grown-ups gathered together again.

'I heard from the Red Cross this afternoon,' Connie announced. 'They've got a group of refugee children going off to France in a couple of days. I don't want to sound brutal, but there's really no point in putting off the moment of Hugo's departure. It's going to be a wrench for the children, anyway, so I think I should take him to London with me tomorrow . . .'

34

The rose garden

Nobody told Holly. Nobody told Holly that Hugo was going to leave that very day.

After breakfast next morning her mother just said, 'I want you to go over now and join Imogen who's helping Grandmamma with the packing.'

When Holly came back she went upstairs to tidy herself for lunch. Through the open door she saw Hugo standing by his bed.

'Hello,' she said.

'Hello,' said Hugo.

Then she saw the small neat piles of clothes and the old battered suitcase.

'What on earth are you doing?' she asked desperately.

'Packing. This afternoon your aunt is taking me to London . . .'

'Oh, no! Oh no! What for? Where are you going?'

'To France, to my aunt,' said Hugo.

'Do you know her?' asked Holly.

'No,' said Hugo. 'Do you know where Nice is?'

'No,' said Holly. 'But I could find out. I could look in my atlas.'

'It doesn't matter,' said Hugo.

'I wish you didn't have to go,' said Holly. 'I wish you never had to go.'

In silence the two children stared at each other.

Then Hugo bent to his packing and Holly went to the bathroom, and locked herself in.

Tears poured down her face, streaking the grime from her work with Phoebe.

As fast as she splashed cold water on her eyes and cheeks as fast again the tears ran down.

Kitty had been standing at the foot of the stairs listening.

Now she ran up to the bathroom and called out, 'Holly! Let me in, darling! Let me in!'

After a while Holly unlocked the door and flung herself into her mother's arms.

'Holly, are you all right? What is it? Tell me, darling. What is it?'

'Oh, Mummy, Mummy!' sobbed Holly. 'I can't bear it! I can't bear Hugo to go! He is my forever friend! Why can't we keep him? Couldn't you and Daddy adopt him? Wouldn't you be happy if you had a boy again?'

Kitty's eyes filled with tears.

'Oh darling, no,' she said softly. 'It's not like that and

besides – I've got you. My own child . . . And Hugo's aunt will need him and he will need her – they have lost everyone!'

'Oh Mummy, Mummy, we're so lucky . . . we've still got each other – you, me, Daddy. Think of Hugo without his parents! Think of Grandmamma and Granddad without their son!'

Kitty's arms tightened round her daughter.

'Yes, darling,' she murmured into Holly's hair. 'I do, I do, I think of them often – very often . . .'

'My little brother,' Holly said bravely, 'he . . . he would want us to be friends, wouldn't he?'

'Yes, Holly,' said Kitty, 'yes, yes, of course he – of course Timothy would.'

It was the first time Holly had ever heard her mother say his name.

'Dry your eyes,' said Kitty, 'while I dry mine. It won't help Hugo to see we've been crying. And now go and call him down for some lunch . . .'

When it was time for Hugo to leave Hereward gave him a five-pound note in an envelope.

Phoebe gave him a copy of *The Wind in the Willows* wrapped in pretty paper preserved from Christmas. 'Something to read on the journey, to remind you of your life in England.'

And she kissed him swiftly, secretly longing to hug him tightly.

Robert Pendleton shook him warmly by the hand. He had thought of giving him a carving tool from his own set, but it no longer seemed a kindly or suitable gift.

'Well, then!' said Guy. 'Best be getting along! Come on Holly! Imogen! Hugo! Make your *adieus*!'

Imogen put out her hand and Hugo took it.

'*Auf Wiedersehen*!' she said firmly.

'*Au revoir*,' said Hugo, keeping to the end his vow never to speak another word of German.

He turned to Holly.

'Goodbye,' said Hugo. 'Goodbye, Holly.'

'Goodbye,' said Holly in a small voice.

Somehow they managed to smile at one another.

It was only when Kitty kissed him, quickly, awkwardly, that Hugo very nearly cried.

'Break it up! Break it up!' said Guy jovially enough, 'Or you'll miss the train!'

That evening the family all had supper together in the large dining-room of Marlowes House with its French windows open on to the wide lawns.

'Well!' said Guy. 'Isn't this nice! A family reunion!'

A heavy silence followed.

'What's up with you?' he asked Holly. 'I've been watching you, pushing your food all round your plate.'

'I'm not hungry,' muttered Holly.

'Not hungry?' repeated Guy.

Holly stood up abruptly, knocking over her tumbler of water.

'How can you?' she exploded. 'How can you sit there, eating?'

'Holly!' Kitty protested, but rather feebly. 'You mustn't speak to your father like that.'

But Holly had not finished. She stared at the pale faces in the dusky light of the dark-panelled room. The Marlowe ancestors stared down in their gilded frames, indifferent to her, to them all.

'I don't understand grown-ups! I never will! All I can think of is Hugo and his parents. They're dead. Dead. And you're all sitting here eating your supper as if nothing had happened. And now he's gone – you've let him go off to live with someone he doesn't know, in a country he doesn't know, where they speak *another* language he doesn't know. And he'll have to start all over again. Everything! All over again!'

'Holly!' murmured Phoebe.

'We can't all go round wearing our hearts on our sleeves,' said Guy, trying hard not to be angry.

'Why not?' demanded Holly. 'Why not? Next thing you'll be saying, "Life goes on. Life goes on." I've heard you saying that all round the house these last few days.'

'Well, it does, you know,' said her father.

Holly ignored him, because she knew it was true and she just couldn't bear it.

'I don't care!' she said. 'As soon as I'm old enough I'm going to go and find Hugo. We're going to write to each other and I'm going to find him and Imogen's coming with me, aren't you, Imogen?'

'Of course I am,' said Imogen stoutly.

Suddenly she was on her feet too.

'I'm not hungry either,' she announced. 'Come on, Holly, let's get out of here. Let's go to the rose garden.'

They clattered their chairs on the oak floor and stumbled together out through the open doors.

For a long time Holly and Imogen walked in the rose garden, with their arms round each other.

'Can you smell that lovely smell?' said Imogen. She bent and breathed deeply into a pale yellow rose.

Its petals were few but wide, the stamens powdery and generous. The stalk was very short and close to the thick, vicious thorns.

'Mm,' breathed Imogen. 'Delicious! Smell it, Holly, smell it!'

Still smarting and raging from the scene in the dining-room, Holly obeyed, but reluctantly.

Then it all came flooding back: she was with Phoebe and Hugo in the garden and Phoebe was saying . . . what was she saying? 'The rose grows close to the thorns . . . oh, so close. Of course, it won't last, but how beautiful while it lasts . . .'

Holly did not feel comforted in the least. At this moment she wanted things that lasted. She wanted Hugo to stay with her for ever.

'If we come back here one day,' she said to Imogen, 'this place will look smaller. And it'll probably be full of weeds. Nothing ever stays the same! Nothing lasts,' she added sadly.

Imogen did not answer immediately.

Then she said, 'I think love might.'

Holly looked at her keenly.

'Do you?' she asked.

Imogen nodded.

'Look,' she said. 'Here come Phoebe and Kitty.'

They did not know how long they had been there, but they were waiting for them at the open gate.

Holly began to run towards her mother's outstretched arms.

Afterword

Some of the events in this story are true.

There was a real Miles Nash who flew to Czechoslovakia in 1938 and 1939 and brought out many Jewish children to safety in England.

In 1938 my uncle, Trevor Chadwick, was teaching in the family prep school in Swanage on the south coast of England. He became extremely distressed at the rumours of the increasing numbers of Jewish children in Central Europe whose parents were desperately trying to get them safely away from Hitler.

He discovered that children could leave on condition that they were under eighteen and if their parents stayed behind. He also found out that the children needed sponsors in England who would guarantee to take them in and support them until they were eighteen.

First he persuaded his uncle, the real Hereward, who was headmaster of the school, to sponsor two small boys and flew to Prague with another master to fetch them. They were taken into the school until the end of the war. Horrified at the numbers of children trying to flee, he went back and started working for the refugee organisations set up in Prague by the Quakers and others. The day before the Germans marched into Prague on 15 March 1939, he still managed to get more children out by plane. One of them, now the poet, Gerda Mayer, was sponsored by Trevor's mother, my grandmother, and remains a friend to this day. He then helped to organise getting hundreds of children out by train (some of the Kindertransporte) through Germany to Holland where the unaccompanied children continued by boat to England.

Like all the workers in this dangerous field he took terrible risks: at one time the necessary documents to get the children out took so long in coming from the Home Office in England, he arranged for forgeries to be made which were so convincing they fooled the Nazis, who gave them the necessary official stamp, allowing the children to leave Czechoslovakia.

Tall, blonde and handsome, witty and wayward, he was also an enchanting uncle. He really liked and was interested in children, and played with us delightfully as Gerda Mayer was to see him playing with the little refugees while they waited for their plane. He really did hold a sleeping baby in his lap all the way to England.

When war was declared in September 1939, he joined the Royal Air Force. We never heard him speak about his work in Prague, and he only wrote about it briefly for a book called We Came As Children [Gollancz 1966, edited by Karen Gershon].

He died in 1979, but is lovingly remembered by some of his 'children' who went on to live full lives – although very many of them never saw their parents again.

Jenny Koralek

NOTE:
About 10,000 Jewish children were brought to safety in Britain as refugees.

It would take a year to read out all the names of the one and a half million Jewish children who perished in the Holocaust.